WOUNDED
BUT
NOT DEAD

WOUNDED BUT NOT DEAD

VINCENT LEFORESTIER

Copyright © 2017 Vincent Leforestier

The moral right of the author has been asserted.

Apart from any fair dealing for the purposes of research or private study, or criticism or review, as permitted under the Copyright, Designs and Patents Act 1988, this publication may only be reproduced, stored or transmitted, in any form or by any means, with the prior permission in writing of the publishers, or in the case of reprographic reproduction in accordance with the terms of licences issued by the Copyright Licensing Agency. Enquiries concerning reproduction outside those terms should be sent to the publishers.

Matador
9 Priory Business Park,
Wistow Road, Kibworth Beauchamp,
Leicestershire. LE8 0RX
Tel: 0116 279 2299
Email: books@troubador.co.uk
Web: www.troubador.co.uk/matador
Twitter: @matadorbooks

ISBN 978 1788037 402

British Library Cataloguing in Publication Data.
A catalogue record for this book is available from the British Library.

Printed and bound in the UK by TJ International, Padstow, Cornwall
Typeset in 10pt Times New Roman by Troubador Publishing Ltd, Leicester, UK

Matador is an imprint of Troubador Publishing Ltd

For my Charlove, my Chichi and Matt.

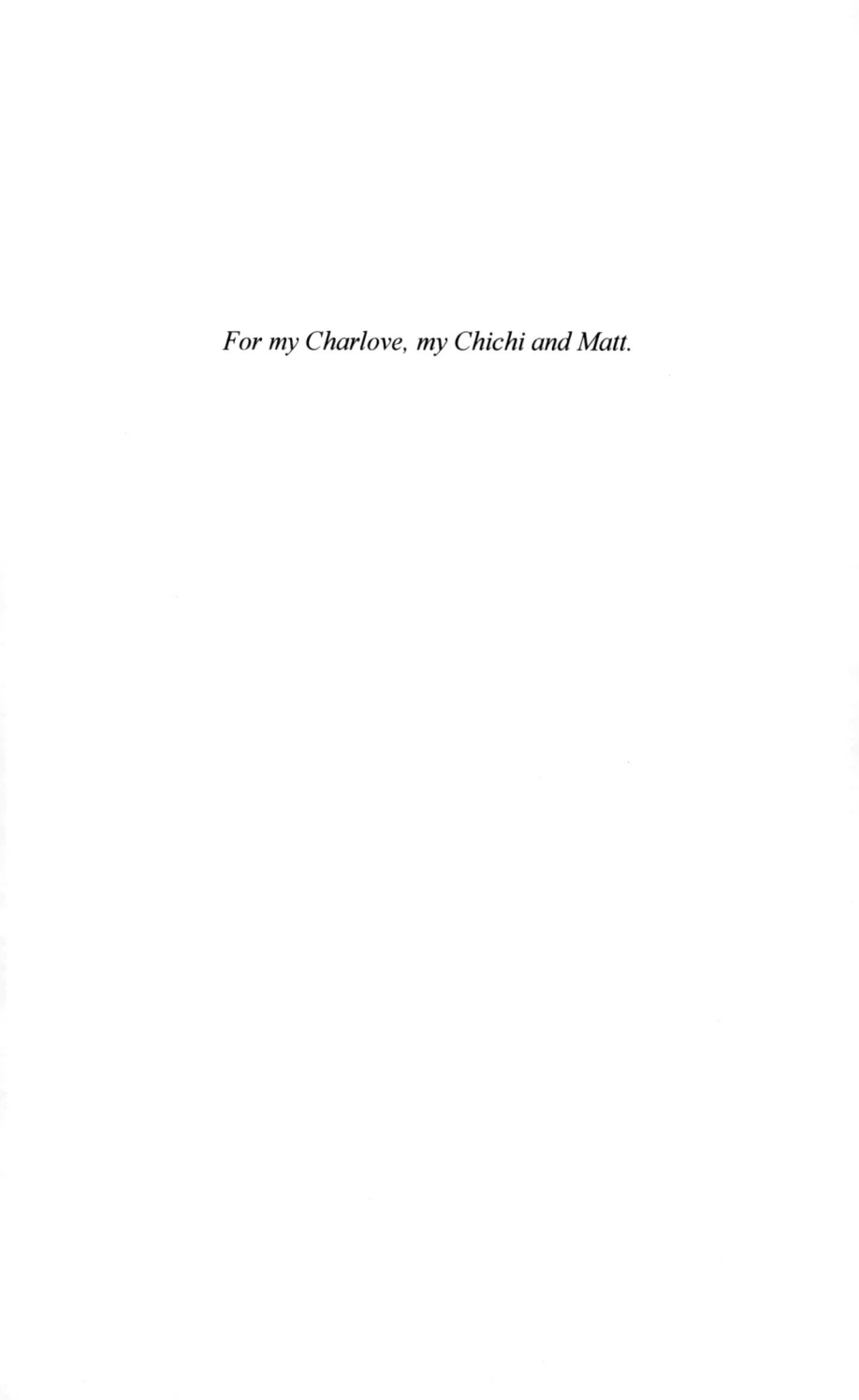

By the Same Author

Le Gouffre
Poetry
Amazon, 2000

Blessé mais pas mort
Novel
Amazon, 2013

PART ONE
BONNY-SUR-GEOY

Bonny-sur-Geoy is a village where life is good. The climate is mild, the land is fertile and the people are happy. You are born, grow up and die there in peace, all year round. In the summer, children play outside; men work in the fields; women cook, gossip in the garden or on the doorstep of their homes and old people dream of their youth as they sit on the benches of the church square.

The summer of 1971 was exceptional. It was Father Moino, the village priest, who told me that.

From July, it was extremely hot. Every day. More than forty degrees. Not a single drop of rain. Restrictions were imposed. A hosepipe ban was put in place. Flowers wilted under the unyielding hot sun. Its rays burned the fields and the crops. Green turned to yellow. And not the slightest breath of wind. The *Bonnygeoyeux,* the good people of Bonny-sur-Geoy, gasped for air night and day, cloistered at home, praying for the rain to come. After two months of scorching heat, their wish was granted. The drought was followed by torrential rain.

It had been raining for a week. It was September 10, 1971. The bed of the Oizot, the river which split the town of Bonny-sur-Geoy in two, overflowed. Flooded roads became impassable.

My mother was about to give birth. It was no longer possible to get to the hospital. Her best friend, a midwife, lived on the other side of the river, on the right bank, where you could find the church, the local school, the bakery, the grocery store and the *bar-tabac*. Despite the appalling weather, she risked her life to help my mother. Unfortunately, she never made it. It was my father who had to cut the umbilical cord. My parents regretted not having chosen abortion. They had thought about it. They could not stand children, but abortion was against the law, and they had not dared. Whether they liked it or not, the thing had finally, and painfully, arrived.

For the villagers, a miracle. For me, the beginning of my ordeal. I had not been wanted. I was an accident, as I would hear them stress so many times, and a few hours after coming out of my mother's womb, I had already been rejected. My mother chose to mourn her dear friend who had drowned on the way. The bawling baby was the cause of this tragedy. On Monday the thirteenth, the rain stopped. The village had been inundated, and while it emptied its ground floors and cellars of the deluge, the village priest came to see my parents. The baby with no name had survived. Father Moino saw in this a victory of Providence. He called me Victor.

1

Saint Yvette

"No pudding for you for a month. And if I hear you whinge it'll be worse."

Guilty for daring to ask if I would receive presents for my ninth birthday.

"Presents! And then what? You make my life a bloody misery. You don't think I'm going to spend money on you?"

"What have I done?" I managed to ask, sheepishly.

"Don't you dare answer me like that!" my mother bellowed in her authoritative voice.

"But what have I d—?"

The sanction was harsh. One month without pudding. I burst into tears.

"No point in blubbering. Go to your room!" she shouted.

Scared that she would call my father, I went to my bedroom. My face pressed into the pillow, I stifled my tears and remained in this position. Exhausted, I fell asleep. My body and my arms turned into three chocolate éclairs. I tried to bite myself, my mouth a few millimetres away from happiness. The more effort I made, the harder it was to get closer to the cakes. I reached out with my tongue but my hands turned into cheese; nausea gripped me.

Earthquake…

It was my mother, shaking me.

"Get up, you lazy shit! Time to bloody well eat! And wipe your face. You're foul."

I had drooled on my pillow. Still numb from my dream, my skinny legs like jelly, I nearly crashed onto the wooden floor.

"If you don't come this minute, there'll be nothing."

Starving, I went down the stairs hesitantly, my stomach in knots. Meals were not an easy task. I had to use my wits to survive them unscathed. I sat down at the kitchen table while my parents ate in the dining room watching television.

For starters, potatoes with a vinaigrette dressing. I hated them. My mother being out of sight, I grabbed the opportunity to put some in my trouser pocket. She appeared suddenly. I held my breath.

"Eat if you don't want your father to get mad!" she said, with some semblance of kindness in her voice.

I complied immediately, accustomed to doing what I was told without thinking.

"More at a time," she continued, in the same tone.

She stared at me through her thick glasses. My mother did not know the meaning of the word love and it was not her way to talk decently to me. She was a small plump woman with red hair and a loud voice who had no qualms about being rude at the slightest opportunity. My father, at one metre eighty-five, was as boorish as she was. He was as thin as a rake, with a balding head, and when he wore his favourite suit, the black one, he looked like an undertaker. The book matched its cover, and he did, indeed, work in a funeral parlour.

I chewed my cubes of potato as if they were chewing gum. I could not swallow the cold and bitter pulp.

"Go on. Put some more in."

She was getting impatient and the tone of her voice had lost what little kindness it had falsely promised, a kindness she normally saved for her garden. Her garden was her passion. When my father was away, she would devote herself to it. She mowed the lawn and pampered her roses of many colours – "the blues are my favourite" – her hydrangeas and all the other flowers, her carrots, her potatoes and her trees from which she would pick fruit. Pears and peaches oozed with juice, strawberries stained lips red while blueberries would turn them blue. She doted on her plants. As for me, I got lumbered with peeling vegetables and, for pudding, if I was not being punished, the only fruits left were the mushy ones.

"You want me to shove them potatoes into your mouth?"

My mouth was full. No more space. I hoped she would leave for a moment so I could spit them all in my hand and put them into the pocket of my trousers, so short that they irritated my skin. She called my father, who hurried in to witness his offspring's ordeal. I closed my fists and contracted my back muscles. In one go, I swallowed the revolting mush. Immediately I regurgitated it, miserably.

"Give him a sponge. Let him clean his shit… I'm going back to the TV."

After mopping up my vomit, I sat docilely under the supervision of my mother, her fists on her hips. Thunder would not have distracted me. She became the walls of the kitchen, walls of stone, where it was dark. A curtain hid an opening overlooking the garden. Open for lunch, not a ray of light at supper. The door leading to the lounge stayed shut. I ate in the dark.

Main course: mashed potatoes with ham. I pounced on it. My mother went out. I managed to get rid of the diced potatoes crushed in my pocket. I hid them between the fridge and the corner. My plate half-empty, she reappeared.

"You threw them up on purpose, so you can bloody well finish mine!"

My appetite, which had revived with the mash, was assailed by about twenty cubes of potato in vinaigrette dressing. As I stood frozen, my dish was then covered with pieces of dry Gruyère cheese. My mother took a perverse pleasure in adding one after another.

"... three, four, five!"

And one more. Every five seconds.

A mountain formed. I felt dizzy. I could not stand cheese.

"All right, just for tonight," she crowed. "Here we go, your pudding."

She took two yogurts and poured the contents on my dinner, which was almost complete. She added sugar "for flavour", a little groundnut oil, salt, pepper, mustard and vinegar "for more taste", and stale bread for "bulk". She mixed it all up: my mother's original home-made speciality, the *purette* of Yvette. She was proud of her mashed potatoes with vinaigrette, and it was probably her self-satisfied air that finally made me crack.

"You want to taste it?"

Surprised by my revolt, it did not take her long to regain control of the situation. A slap stung my face. The force of it made me fall off the chair.

"That'll teach you to be insolent."

Back on the chair, I was force-fed with a large spoon. I hardly had time to breathe before my mouth was filled again with the repulsive mush. There was a stream of retching. I begged her with my eyes to let me take a breath. She persevered. She was not going to stop now. The inevitable happened. I fainted.

Still shocked, I was washed, taken to the toilet and put to bed.

Lying alone in a room furnished with a bed, a chair and a lamp on the wall, I regained consciousness with an empty stomach. I had thrown up the whole of my dinner in the kitchen. I was thirsty. The bathroom was a few steps away from my cage but I was not allowed to go there. I could feel scraps of mash between my teeth. I was alone in a world I did not understand. With no one to speak to, I wanted to die and I hoped that death would take me away. Perhaps if I closed my eyes it would show me the way.

"You pissed in your bed again. Into the shower now!"

I was alive. Death had not shown mercy on me in the night. In an instant I was undressed. My mother pulled me to the bathroom. Cold water squirted from the sprinkler head. Still naked and trembling, I was forced down into the kitchen. On the table stood a bowl of tapioca.

"I hate waste… Lean down this minute and pick up what you hid last night. You think I'm blind? Go on…"

Tapioca with potato vinaigrette nibbled by mice and other nocturnal creatures. Faced with my lack of enthusiasm, she went through the same routine and I was compelled to swallow the repulsive morning porridge. Then she dressed me.

At nine o'clock, I left with my mother. My father was not at home on Sunday morning. He was at the bar with most of the men from the village. Women and children met in the church. That was my only opportunity to see people at the weekend. It was also the only time my mother would hold my hand. We passed the butcher's, the only shop on the left bank of the Oizot, and we crossed the bridge. She chatted with the butcher's wife who, like her, arrived at the church a quarter of an hour before Mass.

"He is very thin, your little one!" she hissed, comparing me to her two chubby boys.

My mother replied that I was a picky eater.

"It is not easy," she said. "We keep telling him he should eat but he won't listen. Like father, like son. His father, he doesn't eat much, either."

Then they made small talk.

"The peace of the Lord be with you always," said Father Moino.

"And also with you," replied the congregation.

"Let us offer each other the sign of peace."

I was dreading this moment. She would kiss me, true to her public role as a good mother. Her bulging eyes frightened me and her lips on my cheek reminded me of the slaps she administered daily. But the greatest pain was to dare to believe that, deep down, she loved me, and that when we left the church, she would be kinder to me.

Pigs fly, don't they?

*

In the village, she was seen as a saint. Once a week she went from house to house with a large basket to collect clothing for a Catholic charity called *Secours Catholique*. This enabled families to receive clothes and meant that I did not have to go to school dressed only in underwear and a vest. We were not rich and neither were we poor, but my clothes were shabby. They had lost their colour. The soles of my shoes were worn out. I had to keep my shorts until I outgrew them. According to her, "a good Christian thinks of others before thinking of himself". Was she a Christian? She knew by heart the words of the hymns. She would pointedly place a ten-franc note in the wicker basket during the collection. She would, with a big smile, shake the hands of the worshippers around her at the sign of peace. She would receive communion with devotion and contemplation.

I once attended a meeting of the Secours Catholique in Bonpomme, the main city in the area, fifty kilometres from Bonny-sur-Geoy. Several villagers had offered to take care of me but it was she who was the Good Samaritan, not them, and she refused.

I found myself surrounded by a dozen benefactors and a boy with dark eyes in a room crammed with piles of clothes. The group leader had congratulated my mother.

"Yvette, I can only admire your dedication. Thanks to your weekly efforts, countless households can put clothes on their backs."

Then she had addressed me.

"Your mum is an absolute gem, my love. Do you know that thanks to her efforts and her donations, I have seen children your age, poor children, smile again? Without her goodness and the goodness of all the mums that you see around you, those children would be cold."

So my mother was a Christian. No shadow of a doubt. She was a saint, the Saint of Bonny-sur-Geoy.

2

Matthieu

The congregation drifted out. Mass had ended. It was all over. Saint Yvette applied strong pressure on the fragile hand she kept prisoner. I winced in pain. My suffering deepened as the journey from the right to the left bank of the Oizot lasted for an eternity. When we finally crossed the bridge, she grabbed my skinny wrist and pulled it in fits and starts. At every jerk, my feet left the ground, my shoulder almost dislocated. I suffered in silence. Noises around me faded, houses became blurred, silhouettes blended into the trees. What was waiting for me on this Sunday afternoon smelled of burning: I was the heretic child pulled by brute force to the stake whom no one would save.

Reaching our destination, I was ordered to get changed. Then she pointed to the garden. On the grass lay an old tatty blanket, on which I would eat a piece of stale bread and a Gruyère crust for lunch.

The barometer pinned against the wall pointed to thirty-five degrees. It was the end of August 1980 and it was hot and dry. As my old vest, my shirt with shrunken sleeves, my button-less trousers, my shapeless jumper and my woollen socks with holes did not completely cover every part of my body, I was ordered to put on a cap, a scarf and gloves "so you don't get sunburnt". The well-polished Sunday loafers that must not be damaged – "for the love of God" – were replaced by my trusty plastic sandals. Dressed in that way, I was ready to face the sun.

These sandals had particular significance for me. I hated them because they were ugly and uncomfortable, but they also reminded me of my holiday, the chalet, the friends, the beach, the sea, this vast expanse of water teeming with sharks, like in *Jaws*. Each year since the age of five, I had been sent to holiday camp with old-fashioned clothes in my suitcase together with sandals. The ones I was wearing were the same I had had on my feet a month earlier.

*

A pat on the head. The group leader was counting the young vacationers. Little Nichard was missing... We waited. The parents and their son finally arrived, breathless. They placed him on the bus, tenderly kissed his forehead, his cheeks, his teeth, his wet eyes. There were floods of tears, hugs. Little Nichard struggled for fear of never seeing his mother ever again, who herself was delaying the final separation. The group leader cut short the display and wished them a good holiday. Final headcount. She put her register away. Everybody was there. A gesture to the driver. A purr of the engine and a last farewell from the children. I looked at my feet. I ventured to peek out of the window, in case there was a last-minute hitch, my mother changing her mind, stopping the bus and taking me back home by force. Little Nichard sat next to me in a row in the middle of the bus, and he was still sniffling when I felt my breakfast rising up. I vomited on his shorts. Whiny, as he was to be renamed during the holidays, was overwhelmed. One of the group leaders came over to help me. My annual thirty days of freedom could begin. Bonpomme and Bonny-sur-Geoy were already far away.

"Should we go and catch some lizards?"

Matthieu, in a white polo shirt, was almost nine years old like me. I followed him.

"The lizard tails bring good luck and they also grow back," he assured me, eyes sparkling with excitement. "It's my dad who told me."

The poor lizard struggled. Matthieu cut the tail in half. I kept my treasured half in the pocket of my skin-tight shorts.

"Do you want some *Carambars*?"

Sweets... Instinctively I looked around as if I had done something wrong. Like all children, I loved them but hardly ever got any. Sometimes I would manage to pinch one or two from the village baker when she turned to the two baskets of bread to serve a customer, but the real joy was to give her a coin, fill my school bag with sweets and have a feast in the school courtyard. For this, I had to steal money from my parents, and I still remembered my last attempt, three months earlier, which had not turned out as I had hoped.

*

It was around 10pm and, as every night, my parents had just gone to bed. I put my ear against the door of my room. When I heard them snoring, I gently placed my hand on the handle and lowered it slowly. I pulled the door towards me while keeping the handle down. Then I held back the upward movement for a long minute during which I let it rise one millimetre every second. I was aware of the risk I was taking and the thrashing I would get if my plan did not work, so much so that at the slightest scare I would be back in bed, eyes closed, as if nothing had happened. A change of pace in their snoring, a rustling of sheets, a curse breaking free, a lamp switched on and I would be under the covers, my heart beating wildly. Once in the hallway, I passed the open door of my parents' bedroom, hugging the opposite wall. My hands were sweaty, the soles of my feet stuck to the floor. I held my breath. Beads of sweat formed on my forehead. Convinced that by dripping to the ground they would wake my mother, I stopped, wiped them away with my fingertips, making sure that my joints did not crack. I could still backtrack but the thought of buying dozens of sticks of chewing gum at thirty centimes each made me grasp my courage in both hands, walk to the stairs and creep down on tiptoe. If my mother got up, I would not have time to retrace my steps without getting caught, so I accelerated. Her bag was downstairs in the hall under the coat rack. I took two ten-franc coins and I went back up with fear in my stomach. Back in my room, I opened the window. I threw one of the coins into the night, aiming at the hedges at the end of the garden behind which there were fields and through which I would put my hand the next morning to get my hard-won possession. I hid the second coin between my mattress and the bed slats and went to sleep. The next morning, I behaved like an obedient child in order not to attract the attention of my mother and I did exactly what she told me to: "Stand up! ... Get dressed! ... Sit down! ... Lie down! ... Eat up!" Except that, as I was going to leave, she stood in the way: morning roadblock. She examined my pockets and my school bag with a fine-tooth comb, and then made me take off my shoes and my socks.

"Spread your legs! Your arms! ... Open your mouth!"

She felt me from top to bottom. A thorough search, but it did not succeed. I had hidden the coin in the toilet. Claiming an urgent need, I went in, slipped it into one of my shoes and went out. When you have nothing and you have the opportunity to have something, you always want more. So I went round the back of the house to get my other coin and maybe more coins that I had not found on previous occasions. Schoolboy error! I had my nose in the hedge when suddenly I felt myself pulled back violently. I had been followed. She had caught me red-handed and, to make matters worse, she leapt upon two other muddy coins which, she guessed, "didn't get there through the workings of the Holy Spirit". She also found the one I had hidden in my shoe.

"I knew that you were a low-down thief. Now go to school and you'll see what you're going to get when you come back. You are going to go through hell, I promise you that."

Two slaps and a kick later, I ran off, with reddened cheeks. I was unable to concentrate in class. I thought about running away, leaving the village, the region, the country, the earth, but without money and knowing little about life, I went back home with my tail between my legs. My mother was waiting for me outside the front door.

She pulled me by the ear, forced me to undress. Stark naked, I awaited the return of my father in the living room, arms in the air. As he was held up at work, I remained in that position for a good hour, until I no longer had the strength to maintain it.

"You're bloody lucky. Your father's coming back late. He'll give you a thrashing when he gets back. Now you'll write 'Thou shalt not steal. This is a sin' two thousand times. And make sure there's none of them spelling mistakes…"

As if she knew much about spelling. Her speech was riddled with mistakes. As for correcting mine, she was more likely to add more. I spent the rest of the evening copying the sentence, and on top of a painful arm, shoulder and back, it was now my fingers that made me suffer. As for the beating, I received it before going to bed.

Such suffering and humiliation for a few sweets!

*

I shoved Matthieu's Carambar into my mouth furtively.

"Everyone line up," a group leader said warmly. "We're going to guide you to your rooms. We'll help you unpack your suitcase into your wardrobe, and when you're ready, you'll follow your leader."

I found myself in a dormitory of eight – Matthieu, Whiny and five others – on the second floor of the chalet, above the big kids' dormitory, the ten- to twelve-year-olds. The leader who looked after our group was a tall West Indian man full of energy named Felicien. "When you're ready, we'll have afternoon tea on the sports field," he said in a cheerful voice. "Don't forget your sun hats, the sun is very hot."

Fresh bread, fluffy brioche, rectangles of salted butter, capsules of strawberry jam and Nutella, marzipan, condensed milk tubes, pomegranate cordial and as much water as you wanted. I stuffed myself. Then we played a game of football. The three girls in the group chatted, lying on the grass, while the boys showed off their sporting skills. In my first match, I coped quite well and I even managed to score a goal. Matthieu and my teammates congratulated me. I got caught up in the game, I felt exhilarated. I would sprint, fall, get up and tackle Whiny. I gave it everything I had. I was doing what most kids in Bonny-sur-Geoy did every Saturday afternoon while I was locked in my bedroom. I was banned from doing sports but my mother never told me why.

*

On the first Saturday of spring there was a running race in my village. The year I turned eight, the event coincided with my mother's hospitalisation for liver problems. As she refused to see me in the hospital, I was freed from the family yoke. I could now take part in the competition. Freed, I started the race at a fearsome pace, leaving behind the other competitors. Carried by my enthusiasm, I ran faster than the speed of light. The sprint for the finish could not have been better, accompanied by the applause of an astounded crowd assembled from neighbouring villages. I crossed the finish line with hair flying in the wind, victorious, and was rewarded with my first helicopter flight. I was not allowed to enjoy my prize: it brought happiness to another child, less fortunate than me, obviously. The following year, I was so desperate to repeat the feat that in my fervour I re-imagined the race in the corner of the living room, to the right of the wide-open window, arms crossed behind my back, on my knees, dead still. I cried in frustration.

*

The day after our arrival at the holiday camp chalet, we went to the seaside.

Felicien, who had taken a liking to me, stood beside me at the water's edge. He kept a close watch on the overexcited children splashing a few steps away.

"I'll teach you to swim. It's easy."

With Felicien, everything seemed easy. We played bat and ball, frolicked on the beach, made sand castles that the rising tide submerged. End-to-end activities. Back at the camp, we played dodgeball, jacks, kick the can, bulldog, treasure hunt, and more games of football. I played so well that the team captains fought to have me in their team.

"The mail… Paul, here are your three letters. Matthieu, you have a parcel. It is in my room. Jean…"

Joy could be read in the eyes of my holiday friends. The leader carried on.

"Pierre. Your parents called. They'll call you back tonight."

I must have looked baffled, since Felicien tried to reassure me: "I am sure your family thinks about you. You'll receive a letter tomorrow."

But there would not be any letters, neither the next day nor any other.

The night before our departure, the camp director summoned me to his apartment, which was on the top floor of the chalet. We had had a pillow fight. Mr Jadu wanted an explanation.

"Wasn't me who started it," I snivelled.

"Who did then?"

I kept quiet. I could not name names – I was not a sneak. I noticed that the buttons on Mr Jadu's shirt were not closed, showing a hairy chest. At catechism, we were taught about Adam and Eve. The director was living proof that man was descended from monkeys instead.

"Who did then?" he repeated. "If you don't answer me, I'll have to talk to your parents."

I began to cry.

"Don't worry, mate," he said softly. "I also did some silly things when I was your age… Do you like summer camps?"

"Yes…"

"I heard that you didn't receive any letters from your parents. Is that true?"

"Yes."

"You want to talk to me about your parents?"

Naively I opened up to him, telling him about the treatment they put me through. He changed the subject abruptly.

"Would you like me to give you ten francs?"

With ten francs you could buy anything! Having no pocket money, I said yes. Slouched in his armchair, in his musty old room, he beckoned me closer. His hairy hand went into my pyjamas and he touched my private parts. Petrified, I let him grope me. Then he sent me back to my dormitory where calm had returned. I put away the ten-franc coin and did not speak to anyone about what had happened. I felt ashamed and happy at once. I used the ten francs to buy two photos from the end of holiday show of me and Matthieu both disguised as shepherds.

Promising to write to each other every day, Matthieu disappeared forever in Bonpomme car park, where parents had been waiting impatiently for their little cherubs.

*

I was thinking about him, sandals on my feet, in the scorching heat, on this blanket which a dog would not have wanted even in the shade.

The sun was beating down so hard I was sweating copiously. Time seemed long in this flowery garden. Only child, no one to play with, no toys. With a dry throat I gave in to memories of the last month spent at the seaside. A rough voice brought me back to reality.

"You're thirsty?"

I nodded shyly.

"Well… so am I."

I heaved a sigh of relief. I would not die of thirst. When my mother returned, she was holding a glass and a bottle that the sun prevented me from seeing properly.

"No more water," she blurted out.

She filled her glass and drank it down in one go. It was whisky, her Sunday drink.

"You'll drink when you won't piss in your bed no more."

"I'm thirsty," I begged her.

"Shut the fuck up," she bellowed. "You won't drink. You'll stay there till *sut*… The sut. The sun. Which sets… Oh screw it, I'm going to bed."

Finished, she took two steps back. The glass and the bottle floated through the air. She lost her balance and fell miserably backwards at the foot of a pear tree, dead drunk. I remained motionless on my blanket. She did not allow me to get up and I did not want to incur her wrath. She curled up in a ball and then lay still. When she started to snore, I made my mind up. Thirsty, I ran towards the glass door leading to the dining room. She had everything planned. Despite being drunk, she had had the presence of mind to lock the door. My search was unsuccessful. I was condemned to the hope she would wake up and take pity on me. I could not count on anybody. We had no direct neighbours. The nearest lived on the other side of the street. On the garden side, on the right and on the left, there were only fields.

Back to life, she got up, lurched into an incomprehensible monologue, took the key out of her bra and walked off in a zigzag, abandoning me once again to the heat of a beautiful and sunny Sunday.

It was only when the rays became less strong that she deigned to bring me some water…

…in a bucket she poured over my head.

3

Geneviève

I hated her. I brooded over my hatred for hours and hours locked up in my bedroom; abandoned in the garden; during the sermon of Father Moino that warmed the hearts of believers but that I could not hear; on the benches of primary and secondary schools: wherever I had to go. It was only when I thought about my holidays with my July Buddies, as I had come to call them, that I managed to temporarily shake off this bad seed growing inside me. I could see us ringing doorbells; throwing chewing gum on towels left unguarded for a moment by keen sunbathers; pinching sweets and chocolate bars from the holiday camp shop, running away as fast as we could once the offence had been perpetrated. My vindictive impulses vanished. We shared our possessions, our strengths, our life. We were one.

One day someone started playing "My dad says…" At that point, I was lost. I did not grasp the concept. My father never said anything to me. He did not speak to me. He struck. Punches in the face to teach me manners. Knee strikes in the balls to remind me that one day I would become a man. Kicks on my body, as I lay on the floor, to make me understand what respect meant. He expressed himself in that way. A mentor with demonic strength within him who rubbed his knowledge in by force. He corrected my mistakes, dished out the sentence and hit. He put so much effort into it that sometimes he cut my eyebrow. My tears mixed with blood, he would hit the curled-up body once more, for form's sake, then phone the butcher who would put in stitches. The butcher did not ask questions. He would also beat his children. After closing the wound, he was offered a plate of cold cuts accompanied by a good bottle of red wine: matter closed, nothing had happened.

Gut reaction to this?

My surgeon returned home. In the night, shutters closed. One neither sees nor hears anything in Bonny-sur-Geoy, the village where life is good. Cheers.

Any arguments?

A good slap never killed anyone. My father the undertaker could prove it. When Ivan Vimord was neither burying a corpse nor slouched in his armchair watching television, he instilled his vision of life in me and still I was not dead. I showed up at school the next day with a swollen face and a stitched-up eyebrow, but alive. I got through the discussions of the playground limping. I screamed in pain at every pat on my back on the stairs leading to the classrooms. I hid my swollen lips – the butcher of Bonny-sur-Geoy, pioneer of cosmetic surgery – in the palm of my hands, elbows on the table and on my exercise books. I isolated myself in the playground during the morning break. Teachers told me to pay more attention when cycling. The pan was of course responsible for my black eyes as I gazed at the ceiling. Bruises on my legs and arms? Naturally clumsy, I bumped against wall corners and against chairs; I even bumped against the foam couch. The unlucky boy to whom all misfortunes happened. The most outlandish explanations were enough to satisfy the few adults who questioned me.

"Skeletor, are you hungry?"

I was faced with the pupil who liked to be called Hogan, the tough guy of Bonpomme's secondary school, a full head taller than me, a yellow band around his head, long hair, proudly wearing a Led Zeppelin T-shirt, a pair of white Adidas trainers and a Lacoste tracksuit bottom.

"You want to stuff yourself with crocodile?" he continued, arrogantly sticking out his chest, a finger on the logo embroidered on the thigh of his tracksuit, under the admiring gaze of his troop.

I had dealt with him in my second year at Guillaume Tell Secondary School. Intimidated, I had not flinched. I was now in my third year and was not going to get pushed around. Full of hate, I lifted him, squeezed him into a bear hug, choked him and then flattened him on the gravel of the playground. A whistle blew. The supervisor intervened and we were sent separately into the office of Mrs Vermur, the member of staff responsible for discipline.

She was a woman who had seen it all before in her school, uncompromising on matters of behaviour. Being called into her office had consequences in the following years of school, and many students emerged from her office despondent. Parents were made aware of the matter; repeat offenders would be excluded for three days; the incorrigible ones would be expelled for good.

The supervisor closed the door behind me. I remained standing.

"Victor, I am waiting," Mrs Vermur said, nose in her files.

"Hogan started it."

She frowned, looking at a list.

"Hogan? But there is no Hogan at the school."

"I didn't fight then."

She raised her head sharply.

"Insolent on top of..."

She stopped at the sight of my injuries.

"What happened to you?"

"Nothing," I replied dryly.

Since Mr Jadu had taken advantage of me at the holiday camp, I had not trusted adults. She did not press the matter. I only received a warning. She had guessed that I was an abused child but, not wanting to interfere in family matters, she became lenient with me.

And I made the most of it. If something was said that I did not like, be it the slightest thing, I would lash out. Towards the youngest and the eldest alike. Until this terrible mistake happened.

Jean-Sébastien, top of the class, had just got a term average of nineteen out of twenty. The best of the best. School report on his forehead, stapled in a moment of jubilation, he boasted once again that he was the best in the school. I kept my composure. The teacher would soon get to me, and the twenty or so students leaning against the walls of the corridor were also waiting for him. As Jean-Sébastien moved closer to me, my marks emerged. Nine out of twenty in English, three in geography, two in history, one in French, zero in civics... Nothing to be proud of, I threw these numbers into the void. But when I heard the strident voice of Jean-Sébastien, who was now a few centimetres from me, my term average, the worst of the worst, went to my head, taking with it my delusive placidity. I made mincemeat of Jean-Sébastien.

He paid for thirteen years of deprivation: no sport, no outings, no music, no cartoons, no birthday presents, no Christmas tree, no hope in the morning. Thirteen years of pain and humiliation in the prison atmosphere of Bonny-sur-Geoy; sunburned in the summer in the cursed garden; squatting in winter dawns on frozen turf to do laundry in a basin of icy water, then standing to hang out the washing, completely naked beneath the sneers of my mother.

Jean-Sébastien paid for all these frustrations. His screams emptied the classrooms of their pupils. I would have killed him. Someone tried to grasp me around my waist. I dug my elbow into them. There was a noise. They let go. Blinded by anger, I threw myself onto another shape which came to the rescue of the terrified boy. A punch. Just one punch then I froze. The hubbub of the spectators. I came to my senses. There were two bodies on the ground: Jean-Sébastien and a girl with long, blonde, fine hair. She was almost at the point of death, her mouth open, covered in blood, two teeth missing. The audience, and Hogan in particular, had taken great delight in watching the first part of the show, my opponent not being popular with the crowd, but the final blow was met with disapproval. "She didn't want to kiss you?" one voice in the crowd dared to say ironically.

The girl stretched out at full length was not just anybody. Her name was Geneviève, a thirteen-year-old model student, but, most importantly, and this is where I got it so wrong, the only daughter of the headmaster.

Mrs Vermur could not show any sympathy. The expulsion took effect immediately. From Bonpomme's secondary school, I was sent to Christ School, a boarding school located in the Paris suburbs. It had been recommended to my mother by her group leader from Secours Catholique.

4

Freddy

Full of fear, I put my luggage down on the tiled floor of the waiting room of Christ School, my stomach tied in knots. A freezing draught passed through the bars of an open window. I shivered in my shorts.

"You are not in a holiday camp," the boarders' head supervisor said coldly. "Please take your suitcase and follow me."

We went through a dark, endless, deserted and silent corridor. My suitcase was heavy. I was struggling to follow close behind the man in a dark suit.

"You have two minutes to store your belongings," he said impassively as he entered a dormitory with about twenty metal beds.

He crossed his arms behind his back.

I complied. He straightened up.

"Saturday Mass is at 6pm, supper at 7."

He looked at his watch.

"Mass is now."

I passed under the crucifix planted in the wall above the entrance of the dormitory, intimidated by a life-size Jesus on the cross and by my status as a complete stranger in a place I did not like and where I would have to spend most of my time. I needed a pat on the shoulder, a sign of friendship. The wish was granted in the chapel where a handful of kneeling children were praying. One of them turned around swiftly, winked at me, then got back to his original position. I sat next to him.

"You're the new boy?" he whispered.

I nodded.

"You can speak. The priest, he's deaf. But when you speak, put your hand over your mouth and don't look at me. He's not blind. If he catches you, he snitches everything to the bastard, the headmaster. He's a twat and he doesn't miss anything. On these benches two hours a day, it's deadly boring."

That face, those dark eyes and short black hair rang a bell.

"Your name is Victor Vimord," he continued. "We met at Secours Catholique in Bonpomme. You were with your mother…"

"I remember…"

He nudged me. I was in the chaplain's sights, who shot. The arrow threw me against the back of a chair. I found myself in an office, facing the man I had seen talking with my mother before she left: the headmaster, a skinny little man with a pale complexion, a crown on his head. He was biting his nails.

"You are from now on in my den, under the jurisdiction of Christ School," he stressed. "Anyone who violates the laws enacted by His Majesty will suffer His punishment."

He aimed a drawer at me and then slammed the rectangular compartment on the table.

"During the service it is absolutely forbidden to speak."

He became more agitated, and the drawer scraped the table.

"There is a set of rules," he yelled, "that you will follow from now on to the letter."

"To which letter, His Majesty?" I asked.

I was as surprised as he was. Before I knew it, the words had come out of my mouth.

He raised his hairy eyebrows.

"To the letter of your choice!" he replied, wanting to know what I was getting at.

"Z then," I continued, unfazed and unable to control my words.

He got indignant.

"Jeez!"

"With a *Z* at the end."

My lips moved but it was not me talking.

"At the end of what?"

"Of *jeez*."

Mr Leffolle, whose first name was Charles, headmaster of Christ School for the past twenty-one years, the absolute master of his domain – at least this is what he firmly believed – needed a moment of reflection. Unwittingly, I did not give him the time to have it.

"Yes, Z," I replied, "z... z... z... z... like a zip! As in Zorro! Me, I am Zorro, the masked avenger. And I have a sword in my shorts."

He panicked.

"Soldiers!" he shouted suddenly. "Soldiers, arrest him!"

The army had abandoned him. There was the sound of a buzzing fly. He glared at it. The fly fell down on the table, dead. Then a long bell rang loudly. I rubbed my eyes, stunned by my audacity.

The headmaster stood up, walked up and down the room, the drawer in his hand. My friend's face appeared in my mind.

There was a knock at the door. This time, it was me who turned my head towards that friend.

Charles Leffolle became exasperated.

"Christian Dubien? You, again...! Don't you know that during—"

"—the service it is absolutely forbidden to speak. Yes I do know it, Your Majesty. But I didn't do anything."

"As usual..."

"As usual..." Christian Dubien repeated.

"What am I going to do with you?" the little man said, discouraged.

Christian winked darkly at me.

"Send us to dinner," I replied, hypnotised.

He mumbled something, checked that his crown was still on his bald head and dismissed us. I saw my friend drop a key in his pocket. The door closed, he turned the key quietly in the lock, tossed it in the toilet and flushed.

"Charlie can die inside... Come on. Let's go to the canteen."

"OK, Christian."

"Freddy," he corrected me. "Call me Freddy."

That year, all teenagers frightened themselves with a new movie character that haunted their dreams. Freddy sounded far better than Christian Dubien, a name he found ridiculous. As ridiculous as his presence in the school where his mother had sent him after the humiliation she went through at the supermarket in Bonpomme.

"I was nicked with an electric car under my coat by a security guard. It wasn't the first time so they called my mother. Can you picture it? My mother, a group leader at Secours Catholique and me, her son, arrested for theft. And there were a lot of people checking out. Her friends, her neighbour, one of my aunts and all the chicks shopping. You should have seen her. She stood up for me. They showed her the car. She forced me to lie, to say I was going to pay for it, and whatever they said, it was her word, the word of the perfect Catholic mother, against the word of a security guard. Then she asked them for evidence. 'You have a video to prove what you're suggesting?' she told them. They didn't know what to answer."

The next day, there would be cameras in supermarkets all over the world. As for Freddy, he got an umpteenth sermon from his mother, who decided that "enough was enough" and that he would learn to behave within a Catholic environment.

"You know what? I don't care. At the weekends there are things to do. I'll take you to *Kelaindan*."

"Kelaindan, where is it?" I asked.

"Don't worry. You'll see."

We heard the headmaster pounding on the door. My lucidity and Freddy's lack of concern guided us to the canteen, where half a dozen boarders and the supervisor were dining in silence. I ate and drank my fill, then shortly after nine o'clock I fell asleep like a baby in this unfamiliar dormitory where I had a friend.

A friend that I greeted the next day as I was sitting down in the study hall. Grounded every Sunday until further notice. The school did not appreciate having to call a locksmith in the middle of the night. The list of kings of the Franks then of France in chronological order, from Merovech to the Valois, to recite without missing a single one; toilets to clean; repentance in the chapel twice a day; break time spent in the classroom; meals taken in the kitchen alone with the padlocked fridge. We had lunch and dinner after the other boarders, me first and then Freddy, who was starving. In class, we sat in the front row at the foot of the teacher's dais, four desks between us. We were totally separated from each other. Our beds were at either end of the dormitory. We brushed our teeth one hour apart. The order had been given to not speak to us, on the penalty of hanging. We went through the winter secluded, a situation which did not affect me: I was used to loneliness.

But for Freddy, it was a nightmare. He was accustomed to being the centre of attention, shouting louder than everyone else, imposing his law. These months of being ignored made him think hard. He felt so hurt that he could not stop thinking about revenge. The intended victim was a tall blond guy called Augustin. For three months, he mocked Freddy, hoping to break him. Warned that at the slightest incident he would be expelled, Freddy just managed to keep himself in check, his nose in the toilet bowl, under the nicknames of this great clumsy oaf. When the punishment was lifted, the monitoring of our comings and goings eased off. It was then that Freddy divulged to me that the following Saturday we would go to Kelaindan.

"And we'll take this fool Augustin," he said through clenched teeth. "When the others sleep, you get dressed. I'll come and get you. And no questions."

He did not utter a word for the rest of the week, which was unlike the Freddy I knew, the Freddy I had heard on my first day at Christ School boasting about his insubordinations, the proud transgressor of rules: cigarettes banned, he would smoke in the playground; "Line up," supervisors and teachers screamed: he would stay on the side, glaring contemptuously at the other boarders; at exactly 9pm, as they were all in bed, he would be walking at a slow pace towards the sinks for his evening wash, waking up with a slap those who were already asleep. He was not afraid of anything, did what pleased him and spoke about it extensively.

But this new Freddy was taciturn, and deep inside his dark eyes with dilated pupils, I saw fire. I stayed away from him until the day came, respecting his desire to be left alone until then. The excitement of discovering Kelaindan dominated my thoughts. What would happen to Augustin made no difference to me. And yet…

5

Augustin

Saturday, March 23, 1985 – 11pm

I was ready. I could not wait for Freddy to come to fetch me. We were going to run away into the Paris night, escape from that prison that was Christ School, free for a few hours to experience adventures that I imagined would be incredible. Kelaindan was a sinful-sounding word, since it came from Freddy's mouth. The time was coming. Do not sleep, I repeated to myself. Must not sleep…

Fingers clicked. I got up, following my mate to the bed where Augustin was sleeping like a log. With a hand put over his innocent mouth, the boy began to suffocate, opened his eyes. A threatening Freddy told him to shut up.

"You move… I kill ya."

With these words, he took out a knife that he had stolen from the kitchen and had shown me a few days before. He put the serrated blade against the throat of the petrified kid.

"Want me to slit your fucking throat?"

Augustin had no intention of dying. He did what Freddy told him to do. He took off his fancy pyjamas, dressed hastily, took his shoes, held out his wrists for Freddy to handcuff him, then we got out of the dorm under the disapproving eye of Jesus, to whom Freddy addressed a satanic salute, index and little finger extended, the other fingers folded back. In a moment we were in the street.

The streetlamps were out. The bells of a church pealed twelve times; a black Golf with darkened windows was parking along the kerb.

"My cousin," said Freddy, "he'll take us to Kelaindan."

Augustin, the studious pupil, could not make anything of the name.

"Where are you taking me?" he said, worried.

Freddy gave a sharp pull on the handcuffs: "Who's talking to ya?"

He finished his phrase with a slap on the back of our prisoner's head and I rushed into the smoke-filled vehicle.

The young driver had the engine revved up. The Golf started straight away. Augustin was sitting between Freddy and me.

The driver had no respect for traffic rules. At every crossing, every stop, every traffic light, Augustin would scream and close his eyes. Annoyed, Freddy blindfolded him and pushed a filthy handkerchief into his mouth.

We slowed down suddenly. The vehicle lined up alongside a van whose lights shone on a group of people sitting in a circle at the edge of a wood. We left Augustin on his own in the car. I questioned Freddy. He answered that we had not yet reached our final destination, but this was their meeting point where they would sort out everything for the night. "They" were four teenagers who gave me a foul look. Freddy reassured them: I was his mate from school.

They introduced themselves, torch in hand. Druggy, our driver and the youngest of the gang, a skinny boy with high cheekbones and a childish look; Boozy, with a purplish puffy face.

"Yo," said Dosh, getting up. He sported a classy suit and a Lorex gold watch that sparkled under the lights of the van. Then it was

Punter's turn, with three stripes on his tracksuit, to pick up the torch. With a jerky movement starting from his right hand to the tip of his left hand, he passed the current to the oldest of the group, Dodgy, who, though close to me, gave the impression of being far away. I took my place between him and Druggy, who was smoking a cone-shaped cigarette. There was Freddy and Boozy sipping some sort of alcoholic drink, Dosh checking through a wad of five-hundred-franc notes, Punter making quick back and forth thrusts between his open fingers with a sharp knife that he drove briefly into the ground.

Dodgy, back from his dreams, talked first: "What's on for tonight?"

"Tall blue-eyed dude," answered Druggy, smiling from the corner of his mouth.

"A fool," threw in Freddy.

"Bet my right hand he's blubbering right now…" Punter was excited.

"Wanna bet?" asked Dosh.

They moved towards the car – all except Boozy, who filled up his glass. Augustin, blindfolded and gagged, was sobbing. Punter took the notes that Dosh handed him.

"That doesn't tell us what we're going to do with him," said Dodgy.

An argument followed. With the car door open, they talked of binding him to a tree and coming back to fetch him early in the morning. Freddy was against it. The months of vilification he had lived through made it imperative that Augustin should be dealt with at Kelaindan.

"The Grotto," he suggested.

A suggestion that did not appeal to the others. They did not seem to want to burden themselves with one more person. Freddy insisted, looking for approval from Druggy. The latter suggested we vote.

Out of indulgence for the youngest, hands were raised without enthusiasm, including mine. That would be my only contribution of the night. Impressed by these teenagers who behaved like adults, I made myself as small as possible and observed them. Dodgy, the leader, everywhere and nowhere at the same time, talked to all and no one, nodding regularly. He went along with whoever was talking to him. He nodded to Boozy, at whose feet lay bottles of Demon, a mixture of all the spirits in his drinks cabinet, prepared in his fireplace. He was sitting down but drawing closer by the minute to the ground, which he hammered desperately. He had drunk too fast and was still thirsty. "More, more!" he repeated. Dodgy agreed heartily, as he did with anxious Druggy, who rubbed the right side of his nose nervously, sitting, standing, squatting.

He said: "Shall we go now?"

Dodgy nodded acceptance. Druggy went on with his routine, sitting, standing, squatting... Dodgy then agreed to Punter's idea. Punter's drawn face indicated several sleepless nights and, floating with exhaustion, he suggested a visit to a place where the betting was heavy. He eyed the banknotes that emerged from the breast pocket of tall Dosh, who was displaying his cash, standing on the roof of the van.

Dodgy agreed with all, but whenever he was talking to any one of them, he was looking at someone else, so that, when he deigned to ask me what I was expecting from the night, he stared at Freddy, who answered that I had never been to Kelaindan.

"Go, go, go!" shouted Dosh, who owned the two vehicles. Dodgy took the wheel of the van, taking with him Dosh, Punter and Boozy. We followed them, speeding in silence on that narrow road, unlit, through woodland. We saw no other car, no houses, not a sign of life, until we took a right ninety-degree turn. The road did not go further. A field lay in front of us.

I walked last in this night march, with Freddy and Augustin, whose blindfold and handkerchief had been removed. Handcuffs had been replaced by a chain around his neck, more convenient for a cross-country trip. Two high rectangular blocks, without windows, stood before us, separated by a narrow alleyway. We went on. Freddy pulled on the chain leash, at the end of which struggled Augustin, on all fours, panting with his tongue out, scratching himself on the walls. Then a passage opened up into a covered piazza surrounded by concrete buildings, crowded with people despite the late hour. I was astonished by what my eyes took in. I witnessed a blade attack. A knife stuck in his groin, the victim collapsed. People, dressed all over in red, lit up by a torch they wore on their forehead, went on their way, stepping on the writhing body. Someone put the man out of his misery, hitting him on his temple with an axe.

"Welcome to Kelaindan," whispered Freddy in my ear.

"What has he done?"

"Settling scores. That often happens."

"What is the Grotto?" I asked.

He turned to Augustin, who was scared stiff.

"I want to hear you barking. You don't want to be carved up, do you?"

Augustin complied. His timid barking earned him powerful kicks in his ribs.

"Here, animals are trained to attack," Freddy said in a cynical tone. "I want you to bark like an Alsatian. Show your fangs... Fine... Now go on, BARK!"

Freddy pulled on the chain. Augustin stood up again.

"Shit! We've lost 'em!"

Boozy, Druggy, Dosh, Punter and Dodgy had disappeared, and the young crowd was so impenetrable that all hope of finding them again vanished. I was pleased. I did not trust those five yobs, and I did not like Freddy as I saw him now, submissive in their presence, when he seemed to exist only through his relationship to Druggy.

Following Freddy, we made our way through the illuminated mass of red hoods to the middle of the square, over which towered a gargantuan stone statue, headless, tagged with obscene graffiti, the punchbag of the youth of Kelaindan, who spat on it, or hit it with chain-sticks or with their fists. Then the statue opened up its legs and showed an opening through which they slowly disappeared.

Freddy used Augustin's skull as a ram. Stunned by the shock, then pushed into the hole, he stumbled down the steps of a steel staircase going down underground. The leash unrolled at a giddy speed before tightening up again. Freddy clung on firmly to avoid being swept away. Then we went down. The opening closed again over our heads. We found Augustin sprawling on some steps, hardly breathing, strangled by the chain around his neck, on which his torturer pulled to make him stand. His face was bloodstained. He had a swelling on the middle of his forehead. His nose was broken.

"That's to teach you, for disrespect," said Freddy. "You had plenty of fun watching me clean up the bogs. Now it's my turn to laugh."

An elbow jab on the nose made him whine in pain. Then we heard nothing more from him all night. Resigned to his fate, over which he had lost all control at school, he went wherever Freddy towed him in that underground maze of metallic walls, ceilings and floors, swarming with creatures that moved by themselves, with a human shape and a slobbering wolf's mouth that they made roar in a terrifying manner as they saw us. Freddy appeared to be waiting for a move on their part. One of them crushed his hairy paw on Augustin's forehead. The magic worked: the bump vanished, the scabs of dried blood came off, his nose became rounder. Augustin displayed white teeth. His canines grew longer, his ears developed points, he grew hair on his skin: half-wolf, half-man. Freddy, cocksure, did not panic. He swiftly caught Augustin's hairy hand and put it on his own face. He was instantly metamorphosed, then made the same gesture on me. I felt a new skin cover me up instantly. I tried to share my astonishment with Freddy. Instead of talking, I roared. But he understood me and answered with a growl.

"Only way for us not to be noticed. A few more minutes and they would have devoured us. Now we can do whatever we like."

"But where are we? And why do we look like wolves?"

"Coz we've eaten Little Red Riding Hood, that's why," he joked.

"What hood? I didn't eat anybody…"

"Not you. Them. They all did something wrong and they come into the maze of the Grotto for their penance."

Freddy pointed to a door with a Time Out sign on it. We went into the room. He ordered Augustin down onto all fours before the wall, tied the thick lead to the door handle and kicked his arse. To my great surprise, he took off what looked like a mask, showing his dark face, and pulled off the hairy overalls that hid his clothes and hands. I imitated him.

He explained that the creatures we had just mixed with were harmless to their own kind. Above ground, they committed crimes: thieving, raping, murdering. Redemption came to them in this underground. Then they went up again, and did it again.

I told him that I was surprised not to see any adults.

"They are asleep at this hour. And they don't give a fuck about what their children are doing. Best case, it's one less mouth to feed. You think your old folks were different?"

"You may be right about mine. But there are parents who care for their kids. I know some in my village," I answered.

"Those don't live in Kelaindan. They have no idea that Kelaindan even exists, and you'll never see them around here. Now you, when I saw you in the school chapel and I remembered I had seen you with your mother, I saw that you were different, that you had been through things and you wouldn't chicken out. Anyway, you're my mate. That's why you're here with me."

His face darkened. He pointed to Augustin.

"Now it's his turn to pay."

He took off Augustin's mask. Baffled, he raised his head. With a particularly brutal kick, Freddy unhinged his jaw. Bloodied, Augustin lost consciousness. We put our costumes and our masks back on. Freddy unknotted the lead and then slapped him until he opened his eyes again. We went out of the room, back into that metallic and lupine universe. The eyes of the creatures around us showed a hatred that was terrifying. Dragged like a sack of potatoes, his skull banging on the hard ground, Augustin passed out several times, each time revived by a couple of slaps. The fangs of the beasts reminded him that he was a stranger. His face scarred, his right eye pierced through, he would have succumbed if the maze had not come to an end. We had arrived in a suddenly deserted space that had saloon doors all around, with their right-hand panel scarred and a sign forbidding entry to over 18s. When Freddy had pushed the blinds, we smelled a repulsive stuffy smell, a stale stench. I managed not to vomit. Our animal skins melted away. Mattresses on the naked ground, on which miserable shapes sagged, were the only furniture in what looked like a dormitory. One of those shapes rose painfully. It was Druggy in a terrible state. Freddy pulled a syringe, half-full of a greyish liquid, from his cousin's arm and stuck it into Augustin's arm. The effect was immediate. The pupil of his left eye, the only one that still let him see what was going on around him, instantly dilated. His heartbeat accelerated and he moved his head from left to right, up and down, at a fantastic speed. Freddy took the chain away from his neck. Augustin's wings opened and he took off frenetically. The supersonic craft did not go far. He crashed against the silver wall. Stars filled the dark room when Boozy appeared, wandering between the mattresses. He emptied a bottle of Demon on the open-jawed carcass that spouted flames of pain.

Freddy picked up the stray bits and pieces of Augustin and put them roughly together.

"Let's move!" he said. From the wretched dormitory, we passed into a sparkling cave that made me blink. We waded in layers of banknotes belonging to the fantastically wealthy adolescent who sat on the fortune he claimed to have won honestly. We were in Dosh's lair, his pride, his life…

"Work," he said. "I been working since I was in my pram!"

Scores of crooks confirmed his words. He called over to Augustin's dismembered body.

"What's your address?"

As Freddy had not found the mouth, Augustin was in no capacity to answer and had to try several times before he could write his address on a note.

"Time is money!" Dosh was losing patience.

Two of his henchmen pulled the paper away from Augustin and left the cave in haste, dangling the keys of a car.

"Move on!" he ordered us. "I've no time for you."

We hurried into an adjoining room, lit with neon lights crackling over tables where beggars in tatters, dispossessed of all their belongings, were staking the last bits of humanity they had left.

"Place your prayers," said the croupier. Punter seized the opportunity that was coming to him. He grabbed Augustin and put him on a box marked "Russian roulette". The wheel of misery turned in all directions. "Rien ne va plus," went on the croupier. The bowling ball bounced, rising higher and higher as the wheel spun faster. People stopped breathing. The mouldy smell became stronger. Players pissed or shat themselves. With a last high jump, the ball crossed through the fluorescent lamp and grazed the ceiling before falling heavily on Augustin's groin. Squeals of pain. The ball slid, then stopped on the neighbouring box. Punter had lost his wager so a revolver was brought, aimed at the temple of the student from Christ's School, legs and arms akimbo, then the trigger was pulled – and stuck. The croupier lost his temper. "The chips are down." At this moment, Dodgy, grinning, handed a pistol to Freddy.

"Now it's your turn…"

Freddy knew nothing about firearms and could not know that, with a pistol, you lose every time at Russian roulette. Not knowing that his action was irreversible, he pulled the trigger and, fatally, the shot was fired.

Augustin's brains exploded.

His body started in a last jump, then lay still. The room emptied itself of its shadows, the Grotto sank into the ground, the ceiling opened, the high rectangular buildings crumbled, the square vanished from the map – and its inhabitants with it.

Nothing, nowhere, as far as one could see.

Saturday, March 23, 1985 – 11.59pm

We were in the street, under the blinking street lamp, Christ School behind us. I could not quite recollect how I got there. I had the memory of trying not to fall asleep while waiting for Freddy to come to fetch me and then of having a strange and dark dream, but that was all. The bells of a church sounded the twelve peals of midnight. A green Deux Chevaux parked across the street. The driver, a middle-aged woman, wearing a fur coat and red boots, clanged the door of her vehicle. She noticed us, looked at us strangely, and suddenly cried out and began to run. I called up at Freddy. He turned to me. His face was pallid. He gave me an empty look. His mouth was dribbling. His shirt was soiled with blood. He held a kitchen knife in his hand with its wet blade. Scared, I jumped back.

"I fucking slit his throat, that fool Augustin," he said, hysterical. "Slit in his bed. I told him not to move. It made him laugh to see me clean the toilets. This time he didn't laugh. Didn't move."

Then, as if to convince himself he was not just raving, he repeated "fucking slit" over ten times...

Augustin le Fonbou, April 1, 1971 – March 23, 1985

6

Victor

Although I had been provisionally cleared of any involvement in the murder of Augustin le Fonbou, I was not wanted back at Christ School. Catapulted out, I landed in Bonny-sur-Geoy on my buttocks. Changes had taken place in my absence. My mother had rented my room to a student for whom she had converted my gloomy depressing prison into a modern and cosy haven: a double bed; a spacious wardrobe; a desk; shelves of books, tapes, 45s and LPs; a record player; a Walkman; a dual compartment stereo; a tape recorder; a television; a video recorder; a telephone with keypad; a Minitel, a microwave, a fridge. She boasted about having spent a fortune for her student, whom she allowed to decorate the walls with posters. She let me gaze at this stranger's paradise and told me that I would spend a night in HIS bedroom, a room he would get back on his return from vacation. She then made me take out all the objects that brightened up the space in which I had moped around when I occupied it, and I slept on the floor on a mattress protector surrounded by football players ogling the huge breasts of Samantha Fox.

The next morning, my mother pounced on the telephone directory. She had to find me a boarding school urgently, a task she worked at furiously. Her routine depended on it. Unfortunately, she came up against the refusal of schools to take responsibility for a student with a past like mine. Concluding that none of them would accept me and there was no other way than to keep me home, and for an indefinite length of time, she sent me to the garden. She made me pitch a tent that I filled in the evening with tins of flageolets and French beans she had just had delivered. She threw a rusty tin opener at me and then, without uttering a word, went back in and closed the new French window curtains. The message was clear: in this house, where I had always felt that I was in the way since I was born by accident – and so should have never been born – my exclusion was the norm.

This new situation reinforced the feeling that I did not fit in anywhere. Thrown out of Bonny-sur-Geoy, Bonpomme and Christ School; turned down by other schools; no roof over my head: I did not consider myself in the common run of people; I was definitely not one of them.

But above all, I did not think like them. I was the only one to have found it unfair that all the blame had been put on Freddy without taking into account that he had first been harassed by his future victim. For me, the culprit was Augustin. He could only blame himself, wherever he was, underground or in the sky, in Heaven or in Hell; either he had his brains blown to pieces or his throat cut. His death did not affect me.

On this spring night, I erased his face and my time spent at Christ School from my memory. As the stock of tins left me with no room in the canvas shelter, I bivouacked in the open on my tatty blanket.

In the days that followed, I enjoyed urinating and defecating on my mother's favourite flowers. Despite loving them, it seemed that she had her mind busy with other matters lately, because weeds had begun to invade the garden. The imminent return of the student aroused my curiosity, but as the curtains of his bedroom remained closed, I had doubts about the reality of his existence. After a few days, and still with no sign of him, I assumed that my mother had lied to me and that all those objects had been placed in the bedroom to infuriate me.

Left to myself, with enough supplies to survive for months, in a space surrounded by a high barbed wire fence which gave me an electric shock to my one and only escape attempt, I filled my days juggling with empty tins, putting one on top of the other, knocking them out and digging holes with a shovel that was lying around in the garden. From the holes I would pull out insects I dissected and that I would soon hear begging me not to kill them.

My hair, shaved regularly, thickened; my shirt and shorts lost their buttons; grime accumulated under my nails and the toenails of my bare feet; a layer of earth covered my skin. Insects kept me company. Now I spoke to caterpillars moulting in my stomach; to the ants with whom I shared my flageolet beans; to spiders that caught flies for me and that I enjoyed in a sandwich, a French bean replacing the bread. Wanting to get involved in our discussions, a nosy cat got electrocuted.

Without human contact, I withdrew into myself, getting away from a world in which my sense of belonging was hanging by a thread, indifferent by choice rather than by nature to what was happening there. I forged a shield to ward off any potential attacks from the outside world. But with the arrival of warm days, I lowered my guard, unsettled by the memory of my July Buddies, a hallucinatory awareness that coincided with the show I offered myself in an advanced state of savagery well after sunset on the last day of spring.

I was lying on my back on the grass, motionless, as every night, when someone drew back the curtains of the rented room in which a light was on. I saw the woman that had supposedly given birth to me. As I did not move, she possibly assumed I was sleeping. Another shape suddenly appeared behind her. This woman who was not my mother, since I had convinced myself that I had no parents anymore, pressed her face against the window, and in a rough movement that made her lose her glasses, she was penetrated by somebody slightly taller than her but who did not resemble an undertaker. The scene lasted for a few more moments, during which two hands grabbed her breasts. Feeling provoked, a blind rage came over me. I stood up abruptly. Surprised, the adulterous woman held back the thrust of the young man. I thought I saw a sneer on her face. She bent down again and the carnal in and out started again with greater intensity, going faster and faster. I seized a concrete block, went up to the French window against which I threw it with all my might. The glass exploded. I ran inside the house, climbed the stairs six by six, and charged into the bedroom with bulging eyes, brandishing a tin I flung at the stranger, who received it right in the face. He collapsed under the screams of she who did not only lend him a room. As she did not have the time to put her clothes back on, I saw her fat legs. I grabbed the record player and then the television, which I then smashed against the posters on the walls. With my tenfold strength, I lifted the fridge, held it above my head, targeting the sinner. She knelt, begged me for mercy, promising me the earth. She swore she would treat me better; I would get my bedroom back; she would give me money so I could buy anything I wanted to. I did not care about her promises. I relished my triumph.

"And him?" I asked, pointing to the unconscious and naked body with a swollen cheek.

She looked down in shame.

"Do *you* want me to talk to your husband about it?"

I had addressed her as *vous* instead of *tu*, and this formal way to distance myself from her came to me naturally. Nothing bound us anymore. Feeling threatened, she drew back and put her head in her hands as if her world was about to fall apart, staring towards the window. Holding her under my thumb, I let the fridge fall near the student's ears. The crash made him come out of his comatose state.

He instinctively covered his genitals. In response, I ordered him to leave. He disappeared straight away.

I found myself face to face with the woman I was interrogating.

"*You* have a husband. Where is he?"

Confused by the *vous* form, she thought about correcting me, but did not dare.

"Where is he?"

"Er... He's... Er... He's not here," she stammered.

It was blindingly obvious.

"Where is he?"

"Dunno..."

"*You* must know where he is. He is *your* husband."

"Haven't seen him for ages."

"*You* haven't seen him? What do *you* mean?"

"He told me nothing. He left..."

"Where is he gone?"

"Er... The morgue... In Bonpomme."

"And he hasn't given *you* any news?"

She looked embarrassed.

"Call the morgue."

She complied. The phone call did not bring anything new. Her husband had not been seen there for a long time.

"And the butcher, he must know something. Call him."

She hesitated.

"What are *you* afraid of?"

"I had a fight with his wife," she replied.

"What about?"

She thought for a long moment. Alas, her imagination was exhausted.

"What about?" I insisted.

"Er... About what... about things... things of life..." she stuttered.

"What things of life?"

"Don't remember," she finally let out, at the end of her intellectual strength.

"Call her!"

She bit her lip. She was lying. I snatched the handset out of her hand.

"Her number!"

Her hands were shaking.

"*You* tell me what's going on here or I go to all the houses in the area and, I am telling *you*, I will get answers!" I went on, in an authoritative voice.

She crossed herself mechanically. My patience was wearing thin. Her tears prompted no compassion from me and I was about to leave when she caught up with me.

My blackmail had finally paid off. Having no choice, she beckoned me to follow her to the end of the garden, through the grass covered with empty tins rusted by the morning dew. She stopped exactly where I had found the shovel and then pointed a finger at the ground.

"He is there, your father."

The index finger was directed towards the rectangle of earth. She told me about the day that followed my departure to Christ School. She had returned home at night. Ivan Vimord was waiting for her upstairs. He had beaten her for no reason. She had pushed him down the stairs. He had died instantly. She buried him in the garden.

"Victor!"

I woke up, whispering my own name to break the silence in which I had walled myself up since my dear companions, the insects, had also let me down. Shocked by the indecency of my outfit – the last button of my shorts had gone a long time ago – the ants had moved away, spiders had withdrawn their nets hanging over the garden and butterflies had flown away, leaving me alone with the burnt cat.

As a matter of fact, I was where I had imagined I was: in the bedroom lit by a pathetic light. Strewn all over the floor, a mangled tin, shattered electrical appliances, pieces of glass, defeated footballers, and Samantha Fox, ripped from top to bottom, confirmed that there had been mayhem in the absence of the lady of the house.

Yvette Vimord, née Puttere on February 29, 1937, was not there. Neither were any traces of her student. I remembered he had disappeared, leaving his clothes behind and they were nowhere to be seen. He could not have been around when the Victorian storm happened. Nobody else but me could have been there. I went to the garden. It was daylight. There was no corpse under the ground. Confused and exhausted, I went back in and fell asleep on the living room rug.

*

A few minutes earlier, a few kilometres away, Yvette Vimord, dejected by real events, sitting on an uncomfortable chair, had dozed off for a moment.

She saw herself in the North of France, as the youngest of a brood of seven, potato-fed, living with the memory of a father who died in the war. From that time she still bore a deep grudge against her siblings, three boys and three girls, six little terrors for the girl they envied. Accusing her of keeping the attention of their mother to herself, they burdened her with sins she had not committed, bullied her, ridiculed her, belittling her to the status of a slave. They pulled her hair all day long, tore her drawings, hid her exercise books, laughed at her in front of her classmates in the playground and made her do household chores, scaring her with ghost stories. If she complained to their mother, those ghosts would come and get her at night. She did not remember ever having loved them and she had not felt the need to contact them again after having let a young holidaymaker kiss her and then following him to his village of Bonny-sur-Geoy in the summer of 1965. Even the tragic disappearance of her mother, who drowned and whose body had not been found, did not bring her closer to her family. The funeral took place without her. She drew a line under her family once and for all, replacing them with Ivan Vimord, an undertaker, five years her junior. He was a young and quiet man who rarely socialised, slept well, had never been with a woman before her and, most importantly, did not intend to start a family. The perfect companion, in her opinion. He did not bother her. He worked, ate a substantial dinner, drank his bottle of wine in front of the television and went to bed. Nothing fancy. Life was simple. She only regretted that he refused to accompany her to Mass on Sundays, devout Catholic that she was. She had strongly believed in God since her childhood; she would often invoke him in the many difficult moments of her youth; she would not miss church under any circumstances. That is how she became accepted by the cheerful and humble community of Bonny-sur-Geoy, whose apparent happiness she envied. To compensate, she practised in front of a mirror, working the muscles of her mouth, trying to smile as they did so well.

One Sunday, after Mass, she had met Ghislaine, an old maid who took care of her parents. Busy with her midwifery profession, her volunteering at Secours Catholique and her septuagenarian parents, Ghislaine, regarded as an outcast as she was not married, had seen the years pass and, at fifty, her hope of finding a husband had vanished. She followed her path, determined and generous. Yvette admired her courage and knew she could count on her. She had helped her overcome her pregnancy as a mother would have done for her daughter; she had listened to the terrible things she said about children – they were evil, cruel, useless and a waste of space – and she had taken her in her arms many times to reassure her, explaining that her reaction was legitimate but to see her baby for the first time would annihilate the past, convincing her that on the big day she would feel the joy of becoming a mum. When she had drowned on September 10, 1971, Ghislaine took away with her the happiness she spoke about with such fervour, and the wound Yvette thought had healed, the death of her own mother who disappeared in the same circumstances, had reopened. She had mourned for the only two women who had been important to her, tormented by the regret at not having bid farewell to her mother, accusing the thing that was bawling of causing the death of her friend.

Yvette Vimord shivered in her chair, chilled by memories that the present could not warm up. Her husband, lying on a hospital bed, on a drip, connected to an electrocardiograph, hovered between life and death. The day before, in the afternoon, Ivan Vimord, drunk, was hit by a speeding hearse returning from a funeral. The long vehicle had sent him flying over the hood of a parked car. Broken ribs, arms and legs, an unrecognisable face – it was a pitiful sight.

Yvette, tired of staying by his bedside all night, decided to go home to rest, with the intention of coming back later in the day.

Overwhelmed, she went straight up to her bedroom, not noticing her son lying on the living room rug peeking at her. She did not see the chaos in the room next to hers and she would have stayed numb even if the earth had moved, so much did she feel consumed by remorse. She felt guilty for having caused the death of her husband.

It all started with a simple haggling. Yvette, finding the meat overly expensive, picked a time when the butcher's wife was not there to make eyes at the butcher, who, flattered, agreed to sell his goods at a price that he offered to no one else. This did not please Mrs Largrau.

Keeping the accounts and frowning upon the smiles that these two exchanged, she advised Ivan Vimord to keep a closer eye on his wife. Gossip soon began and the rumour that Yvette Vimord was cheating on her husband with Mr Largrau quickly went round the village. Instead of asking for explanations, Ivan took refuge in bars. Before meeting Yvette, he had never had any success with women who intimidated him and he had never dreamed that one day one of them would agree to put a ring on her finger. To imagine that his wife could break the promise she had made in church to always be there for him and to remain faithful traumatised him so much that he was returning home later and later, drinking more and more every time he went out, collapsing on the first floor, at the bottom of the stairs, in the corridor, by his front door, on his way home. Men had mistresses, not the opposite.

For Ivan Vimord, it had been the failure of his life, a failure based on a rumour which was false. Mr Largrau had never been Yvette's lover. She had never had any lover. She could have denied the facts, but in revenge for having been knocked up and then having to take responsibility for a kid, she had let her husband drown in alcohol, with the consequences that followed.

Full of remorse, Yvette Vimord could not sleep. She got up.

*

Hearing footsteps from upstairs, I stood up from the rug, went to the kitchen to take a bread knife and I waited for her.

Heavy footsteps were coming down the stairs. Only five steps left. Countdown. Four. Standing in the living room. Three. Naked and dirty. Two. Knife in hand. One. The phone was ringing. Startled, I dropped my weapon, my mother appeared, and I urinated on the rug. She gaped at her naked and muddy son from head to toe and must have thought I needed a good shower. She bent down, picked up the knife and, to my astonishment, she gave it back to me. The answering machine came on.

"Mrs Vimord," a pressing voice said, "please get in touch with the hospital urgently."

Then the phone was hung up. One long beep sounded in the room. We stared at each other. We looked like two wrecks washed up by the sea, drawing up alongside the shore of their disagreement. Her red and puffy eyes, her drawn features and her rumpled clothes indicated that the storm had also wreaked havoc on the other side of the ocean which separated us. We sized each other up. Pierced hulls, broken masts, twisted rudders. They had their work cut out. Morbid thoughts to evacuate, wounds to heal, dignity to restore. A titanic, pyramidal, lunar crossing. Asteroids, desert, *la mer, ma mère*. A twist of fate and maybe... Maybe they would go, flank against flank, sailing on the waves of the Red Sea.

As if...

The phone rang again. This time she picked it up. The news was in. At the Bonne Chance Hospital of Bonpomme, at eleven fifty-nine, shortly before the lunch service, in the presence of a trainee nurse, Ivan Vimord's heart stopped beating. CPR. For the last time. The shrill sound of the electrocardiograph.

Ivan Vimord April 1, 1942 – June 21, 1985

I felt wronged. I would have liked to have seen him a few seconds before he died. I would have disconnected him. Bread knife in hand, I mimed the scene, pulling the tube with all my strength. Accidentally, the serrated blade slashed the side of my right thigh. Surprised not to feel any pain, I passed the knife over the wound a second time. Painless. Ninety days outside, two thousand one hundred and sixty hours of loneliness, one hundred and thirty thousand minutes as a caged wild animal, and eleven million brushed-aside heartbeats had desensitised me. The third time – as I wanted to be sure – I put more pressure on the handle, brought the blade slowly back, cutting myself deeper. The beating of my heart sped up. The knife fell again. A hand gripped my wrist. A thick hand. I pushed it away with brute force. How dare she think I had forgotten? I felt a tingling in my thigh. It did not even hurt a bit. I kept my focus. I did not need a knife. My mother stepped back. Fourteen years of punishment... From my open thigh, she saw a tidal wave spurting. Bereaved, terrified, condemned to regret having given birth to me, having been fiddled under the effects of alcohol, having followed this man to Bonny-sur-Geoy and having let him kiss her on the beach, she must have thought her end was near. "Pray for us sinners, now and at the hour of our death," she let out before crossing herself. The wave of blood was still flowing.

I could not feel my right leg. Nor my left. My ears were ringing. The grey rotary dial phone. My lips got colder. My mother's lips were moving. I was frozen. The living room spun. A siren, men in white. I was being lifted. Higher and higher. The oxygen was scarce. I was in the mountains, hiking on a steep and winding road leading to the summit.

After losing consciousness, I had been taken to the same hospital where, a few hours earlier, my father had died. Meanwhile, instead of coming with me, my mother had stayed home and enrolled me in a youth camp.

7

Kimpôl

At an altitude of 1,500 metres, the hikers put down their backpacks near a fountain and ate their lunch voraciously. I sat away from the group. I had not uttered a word since the death of my father, evading questions from the doctor and nurses at the hospital and remaining silent at the funeral, during which I did not cry. Now, more than anything else, I wanted to be left alone. Outstretched hands coming at me as a sign of compassion, I spat on them.

Sitting on the grass, leaning against a tree, hungry from the long morning walk, I was devouring a ham and butter sandwich when a deep voice called me by my first name. I scowled instinctively. I did not intend to break the rule that I set myself to not speak to anyone.

"You seem very quiet."

A mouthful of dry bread.

"Did you have your tongue cut out?"

My flask. I was thirsty.

"You must have things to say… We all have things to say."

I munched on a tomato.

"Do you like chocolate?" the deep voice asked me.

The juice dripped down my chin.

"Me, I love it... And when I want some, I go to the supermarket," he said, lowering his voice as if he was trusting me with a secret.

I looked out of the corner of my eye, intrigued by the mysterious and satisfied air with which he spoke about his visit to the supermarket.

"You wouldn't have any chocolate on you by any chance?" he asked.

I shook my head.

"The best is hazelnut. Milka. Mmm... My favourite chocolate bar. I'd do anything to feel a square melt in my mouth..."

What was he up to?

"All in good time!" he said, as if he had read my thoughts. "Let me tell you about my last foray into a supermarket. I wanted chocolate. Nothing strange. I always want chocolate. So I go to my aisle. I take twenty chocolate bars. I tear the packages, shove one bar in my mouth and the others in the lining of my bomber jacket without anyone noticing, and I push open the glass door of the store. That's my routine..."

He interrupted his monologue to sit in front of me, his squared shoulders sealing my horizon.

Dressed in a khaki uniform, wearing army boots, with a shaved head, he commanded respect. His wrinkled face was not familiar to me. I made an effort to remember the other teenagers with whom I had been in camp for the past two weeks and who had failed to break my silence, but nothing came to my mind. I had not paid attention to their faces, not heard the tone of their voices and did not know their names.

"My name is Kim, but call me Paul."

I listened, thinking that I would eat my apple later.

"So I was going to walk back out when they jumped on me," he said. "Three hefty security guards. They searched me. I kept my cool. What could they prove? Chocolate without packaging? I have the right to walk with chocolate bars on me. They didn't come from their supermarket. Sorted. When the cops arrived,

I was relaxed. I even laughed when I saw them. They were so small. Even you, on your knees, you would have found it hard to headbutt them."

Kim, or Paul – or Kimpôl? – burst out laughing but then put on an annoyed face.

"Did you know that there are cameras in supermarkets now?"

I saw Freddy winking at me. A sound came out of my mouth.

"Yes…"

"You could have told me!" he thundered.

"But…"

"Two words, it's a good start," he continued with his fiery voice. "Get up and let's go."

My backpack was heavy. Because I had refused to share a tent, I was carrying a whole one. The weight of the two canvases and pickets pulled on the straps, and with the movement, blisters had formed on my shoulders, making walking uncomfortable. With Kimpôl by my side, I forgot the pain, discovering the hilly landscape, breathing the fresh mountain air.

"You've suffered," Kimpôl guessed.

"That's true," I replied ten minutes later, five kilometres from the summit.

"I'm listening."

"I have the right to remain silent!" I protested an hour later.

"I'm listening to you, *my friend*."

He had said *my friend* in English.

I caught my breath under the one-kilometre banner.

"Why do you want me to talk? You think you're stronger than me?" I said, attacking him.

"I am stronger than you," he said, laughing at me.

He flexed his biceps. One metre ninety, eighty kilos, a martial arts champion: you could rely on Kimpôl if you were looking for trouble. All you needed to do was to pick a quarrel with him.

"What's the point of being stronger than me?"

Two questions, spoken with no hesitation, stamped and franked as if on a postcard and smoothly delivered. Freed, I glimpsed the hope of healing. My wounds reopened.

*

1979

I was screaming in pain.

"Stop, Dad… Please, stop. It hurts…"

"It's not a little bastard like you who's going to rule here in my home!" he bellowed.

I saw the fingers of his hand folding away, his fist closing and gaining momentum. What could I do? I did not understand. I was scared. Scared of being hurt, of reacting. Scared of the rain. Of hail. Of a deluge of spikes.

"Ouch… Stop please… I promise I won't do it again. I swear…"

I implored. I was eight. I did not want to suffer anymore. I wanted to die.

The violence of the blows affected my breathing. I held my lower abdomen, bent double. I cried so much I was in pain. So much I was afraid. I made calls for help, the echo of my voice. Mine only. I begged. I promised. I was on the floor. My spine was stretched. I protected my coccyx. I defended myself. I warded off one attack but not the following ones. I resigned myself. I endured. There was nothing to see, it was not a circus here. Behind closed doors. Between four walls. In Bonny-sur-Geoy, walls had earplugs in their ears.

Kicks with sharp shoes between sobs. No point in living.

After the shower of blows, I returned to my bedroom, trembling. Above my bed there was a wall lamp. I had stolen a shoelace. I rolled it around the square metallic lampshade. A sailor knot. My head in the circle. I wanted to die so I acted. I squeezed. Tight. I choked. I hung myself. My feet wriggled. The reasoning of an eight-year-old boy: if there are only thrashings in life, better to kill myself...

*

"My answers can wait," Kimpôl retorted. "Your story needs to be heard. Believe me. Death is at your heels. It knows that you are weak. It will take you away with it at your next attempt."

*

At eight, then around my tenth birthday and again a year later, I tried to kill myself. Hanging every time. Three failures. The lampshade collapsed; the string hanging from the ceiling broke. My father, an unexpected witness, harangued me while I was standing on a chair, rope around my neck. I was going to jump.

"Do it!"

My legs were shaking in thin air. Almost dead. A nightmare. I saw myself waking up in a coffin. In the dark. Buried alive. "Help me... Get me out of there... I won't commit suicide anymore... Please, Mum. I am your son. You can't let your son rot in the ground... Have mercy on me, Mum... Hail Mary, full of grace... Blessed is the fruit of thy womb..."

Shaking, I got back down from my pedestal. Rather than hanging myself, I would poison myself so I would not suffer. Then I would jump into the depths of the Oizot, the river of my village. The current would transport my body to the ocean and the seabed would suck it up. May my destiny achieve the fate of my grandmother.

*

Slouched, with my hands on my thighs, I thought about my grandmother while crossing the finish line. She lived in the depths of the sea. I almost touched the sky. Between us, there was the reality and the other hikers who were struggling to cover the last metres of the climb. An adult with a thick beard, a tight band around his head, congratulated me, accompanied by a round of applause from the mountains. *La Marseillaise.* A medal presentation. A medal in chocolate. A melting hazelnut Milka. "A delight" were Kimpôl's words as he offered me a bar. My achievement rewarded. The one nobody expected, Victor, on the highest step of the podium. That was a cause for celebration. With Kimpôl, it had to be with chocolate.

Good things come to an end. A glance at his watch, a nod in my direction and he told me we would meet again later, without specifying when exactly, before vanishing under the nose of the adults. His name was not mentioned during the evening, which, exceptionally, I attended. Usually, once tents had been pitched and the dinner eaten, I would have taken off my shoes, lain down in my sleeping bag and been seen again at breakfast time the next day. But on that evening I sat on a tree trunk, around a campfire, cooking potatoes and corn on the cob wrapped in aluminium, moving my hands close to the flames, to the sounds of a guitar, of crackling twigs and firework explosions: an induction into a warm, musical and festive world. I do not remember what I said on that thirteenth of July 1985, but I have the memory of having spoken and been heard. Kimpôl, nowhere to be seen all evening, appeared briefly to wish me a good night. He said he had to leave, swore that we would meet again and then gave me a hug. A sweet feeling of well-being. I existed for Kimpôl. An only son, I had a brother. A one metre ninety national martial art champion older brother.

Was he a figment of my imagination? An emotion gripped me. Human warmth.

8

Elodie

It was a warmth that vanished on my return to Bonny-sur-Geoy. My mother, dressed in black, locked in her grief, restricted our relationship to a minimum. We lived under the same roof, so sometimes we passed each other on the stairs, without looking at each other, she going down, I going up the steps. While my trip to the mountains and the omnipresence of Kimpôl had pulled me out of silence, she had let herself fall into it. She got out only twice a week. As well as on Sunday morning she would now go to church on Saturday evening, muttering incomprehensible things. Every Friday, shopping was delivered to her door. The rest of the week, she either sat on the couch, in front of the space where the television had been, which she had got rid of, or she hid in her bedroom, mulling over the events that had made her a widow.

Overcome with boredom, it was with relief that I saw September approaching. The headmaster of Bonpomme's secondary school, torn between what he saw as a tragedy – "one doesn't lose one's dad every day" – and his powerlessness in getting his daughter's teeth to grow back again, finally agreed to reinstate me on the conditions that I repeated my year and did not go too close to Geneviève. I affected a military attitude and I nodded, fingers crossed as a sign of non-allegiance. I walked around the telescope on a tripod in the new headmaster's office and pushed open the glass door that led into the playground. It was a nice day. A refreshing breeze and cloudless skies. Long time no see... At the appearance of a ghost immortalised a few months earlier by television and newspapers, Bonpomme's pupils froze and turned towards Victor Vimord the killer – doubts persisted in some minds about the death of Augustin le Fonbou: I should have been convicted of complicity and some of the general public liked to believe that I was also a murderer – an orphan murderer. Victor Vimord on the evening news. The announcement of the death of my father three months later on the lunchtime news. My name recognised by millions of people.

"A star", Kimpôl could have said. He would have been proud of my army boots. They were as polished as those that always shone on his feet.

It was the third day of school, the first for me since the headmaster had procrastinated before taking the decision to reincorporate me, giving himself time to move his office to a strategic point from which he could watch my doings while listening to the news on the radio, on the watch for a twist in the Christ School case, whose trial had just begun, and a possible phone call warning him of the arrival of a squadron of police dispatched to arrest me.

The subject of all discussions, frozen since the playground opened itself back up to me, I had, from now on, a status to defend, a celebrity status that not one student from Guillaume Tell Secondary School could challenge. Not even Hogan. None of them had been on TV. They spoke about me all over the country. They spoke about Hogan only in the playground, his playground, his territory. I stood up straight. A glance to the right, to the left. Freeze frame. Groups of two, three, five at attention. I examined the appearance of my troops carefully. How great it was to feel respected! My eyes lingered on Private Jean-Sébastien, whose satchel was open, exercise books and library books neatly arranged. I sniffed him.

Inspected his shoes. A yellowish puddle at his feet, he had a strong whiff of bilge water.

"Order... Arms!" I screamed.

The conversations resumed. Jean-Sébastien's teeth began to chatter.

"Not you," I went on in a commanding tone. "You, you do press-ups."

His short legs were shaking. The rubbing of his thighs against his shorts and the beating of his heart against his T-shirt had concealed my words.

"Press-ups, you know what they are? And while you're at it, clean my shoes."

The blond mane of Hogan's hair appeared from behind the curls of his bleating army.

"I'm not scared of you," he said, gesticulating in all directions.

"*Baa...*" the sheep followed.

I sneered at Hogan.

"Behave, Jean-Sébastien!"

The high-pitched voice of Mrs Vermur, sent by the headmaster, who was watching the scene with his telescope, stopped the hand of the top student, who was about to polish my boots with his handkerchief. Jean-Sébastien, the best pupil during the entire previous school year, despite two months of convalescence, who remembered my whacks, was called to order by Mrs Vermur. Her long tight skirt, beige V-necked cardigan and pointed nose blended into the shrill sound of her voice. Jean-Sébastien sprinted away. Hogan walked away, stamping his feet on MY playground, followed by his flock and Mrs Vermur's high heels. The headmaster was vigilant.

I continued my tour of the playground, sure of my authority, when the beautiful Elodie Chanelle came into sight. I hardly dared to look at her when we were in the same class, not even knowing if she was blonde or brunette, with her turned-up nose and her mischievous almond-shaped eyes. She made me lose my composure.

"Can I have your autograph, please?" she asked me in a smooth voice.

I looked lost. I had no clue about girls.

"What are you waiting for?" a deep voice pressed me.

Kimpôl had swapped his battledress for a pair of black shoes, a suit, a white shirt and a tie.

"She wants you."

I was stunned.

"What are you doing here?" I asked.

"It's obvious what I'm doing here, isn't it?"

"You came to see me…"

"Yes. Right now, I came to see you and talk to you. But in a few minutes, you're going to return to your classroom and me to mine."

"You're in which year?"

"In Year 13."

"Year 13? What do you mean?"

"In my final year before university."

"So you're going to sit the baccalaureate exam?"

"Something like that. Yes."

"But there is no high school in Bonpomme!"

"Exactly."

Kimpôl passed his hand over his short frizzy hair. The buzz cut from holiday was not appropriate for the student that he was. Because he was a sixth-former. For real. He studied sports, biology and psychology, was in the second and final year of his A levels in a secondary school in England.

"In an English school…" I said, puzzled.

"Yes, *my friend*. In London."

Kimpôl removed his sunglasses that would be of no use in the London greyness.

"You're a student in England?"

I gulped. It was impossible for him to be in his classroom in a few minutes. Unless he could be in two places at the same time. It was nonsense.

"You know how to use your imagination. So use it. You call me Kimpôl. In this country they call me Kim. In London it's Paul. Irrational, wouldn't you say? Isn't it the worst absurdity to believe that a child is to be blamed for all misfortunes? That I am at once Kim, Paul and Kimpôl with a hat on the *o*, that I am in England and France at the same time, isn't it more plausible?"

He put a hand on my shoulder.

"And your sweetheart, does she exist or not?"

I rubbed my eyes. Elodie Chanelle had taken off her white blouse, revealing small, firm breasts. Aroused by her hardened nipples, sucked by her fleshy lips, stunned by her vanilla scent, I looked for my big brother in the playground, which was emptying. He had indeed vanished. I felt sad. I had the feeling I would not see him again for years. Feeling nostalgic, Elodie Chanelle snuggled against my body. I surrendered my arms, just for the length of a school break.

"…Victor? Victor!"

I looked up in slow motion.

"The date, Victor, the date!"

I opened my eyes wide, raising my eyebrows so that my eyelids would not close. My forehead was resting on my arms, and I had fallen asleep in class.

"The date!"

Mr Riotte was getting impatient. I looked at the blackboard.

"The twenty-second of May 1987!" I replied, half asleep.

"The date of the German army's capitulation," the history teacher exclaimed. "Not today's date."

Giggles broke out. I stood up and groggily identified the troublemakers. You did not get away with making fun of me.

"Eighth… May… forty-five…" those who had not been able to control their emotions whispered between nervous laughs.

Exasperated, Mr Riotte spoke to the class counsel.

"Could you please take Victor to the headmas—"

"The eighth of May 1945!" I cut him off.

The teacher pretended not to hear.

"To the head—"

"Are you deaf?" I exploded, cut to the quick. "The capitulation was THE EIGHTH OF MAY NINETEEN FORTY-FIVE."

Mr Riotte pointed his finger at the door.

"I won't go," I replied. "You may as well go all by yourself."

The teacher was speechless. In his twenty-five year career, he had never had to deal with such a disobedient student.

*

In September 1985, a year and a half before, when he had learned that Victor Vimord was to return to Guillaume Tell Secondary School, he had protested to the headmaster. A thug had no place in their school, let alone in one of his classes.

"And not just a thug but also a student banned from the school!" he had cried aloud in the nearly empty office where there only remained a table, a coffee maker and two chairs. "You have expelled this thug, haven't you? So how is it that he is back? What message are you sending to pupils? That the authorities don't have any authority? That an expulsion is a suspension? And a suspension, what is it then? An option? I don't understand you. There are rules you have put in place, which are complied with, to ensure that we, teachers, we can do our job properly and there…"

He paused and looked around.

"Are you changing office?"

"I am moving into Mrs Vermur's office."

"Ah! It overlooks the playground… So you can keep an eye on him. Tell me if I am wrong. You change office to keep an eye on a pupil who shouldn't be there. You have made your mind up and whatever I have to say will not change your decision…"

Indeed, his opinion would not be taken into account. So for months, in the canteen, in the staff room, in the hallways, between lessons, the history teacher had continued in trying to make himself heard, breaking into his colleagues' discussions, always returning to the case of Victor Vimord. But his colleagues had resigned themselves and it was as if Victor Vimord did not exist for them. Some had children schooled in Guillaume Tell, others had a life outside the school, and those were good enough reasons not to take any risks and incur the wrath of a loose cannon.

As soon as Patrick Riotte began his diatribe, in a flash, in the middle of a break, teachers would disappear: they had something important to do.

As for the headmaster, he would reply that he had to be patient.

"Why are you protecting him?"

The history teacher was not the only one asking this question. The other teachers, the school staff and parents did not understand what drove a man to defend a boy who had messed up the face of his daughter.

After expelling Victor Vimord, Mr Pinson had been seized by guilt. Given the seriousness of what Victor did, the headmaster could not do otherwise, but his decision had gone against the values he had been taught to defend. Following the Christ School case, he had a long discussion with his courageous Geneviève and then pleaded the cause of Victor Vimord to the rector for him to be allowed to return.

Mr Pinson had not forgotten that he had himself been helped at a crucial moment of his life. What would have happened to him if, at the age of fourteen, when he had just lost his parents, he had not been taken in by charitable, attentive and fair souls? Would he have respected the hierarchy and accepted the rules? Would he have succeeded in his studies? It was his turn to help young people. So Victor Vimord would remain in his school until he took his *BEPC*; then, with or without his diploma, he would send him to a school suited to his needs as a troubled young person. For this, he had made the necessary arrangements. He first contacted Mrs Vimord, who he felt was detached from the future of her son. She had consented without difficulty that he could get in touch with The Manor, the school that had held out its hand to him at the most difficult time of his youth, shortly after the death of his parents, and which had offered him bed and board. There, he had studied and recovered a liking for life during his teenage years. In a phone call, and without having to argue, The Manor had agreed to support Victor Vimord from the start of the 1987 school year.

*

Angered and speechless, the history teacher was still pointing a finger at the door.

"I won't go!" I repeated in a threatening tone.

"Well... I... I'll go myself," stammered Mr Riotte. "And I can tell you that the school will not keep you. Or I'll be the one to leave..."

I did not let him finish his sentence. I left the classroom, slammed the door violently, and on this twenty-second of May 1987, at nine thirty in the morning, I made a V-sign at Guillaume Tell Secondary School and at my diploma. I left the outskirts of the town and, walking fast, I took the country road lined with fields of corn and wheat, deserted since the highway had been built. Fifty kilometres separated Bonpomme from Bonny-sur-Geoy, so I counted that at a speed of six kilometres an hour, the trip would take me eight hours and twenty minutes. Halfway through, I had crossed paths with five tractors. I calculated... One every fifty minutes. The proof that I was not as bad as the teachers insinuated on my school reports. The hours walking on the country road had not been in vain. As a reward, and without further exams, I claimed my diploma for myself in a concert of beeping horns.

The beeping was continuing behind me. I turned around. An old white minibus had stopped. Suspicious, I slowly came closer to an open window. A man in his sixties, with a white crew cut, a thick white moustache and a round face extended by a white beard, was at the wheel. He invited me to sit. I walked around the minibus, which oozed cleanliness, and sat next to the driver in the vehicle equipped to accommodate fifteen people. Two war medals hung on the old man's black jacket.

"I'll take you back home, young man!" he told me in a deep and reassuring voice. And without further ado, he took me back to my mother.

9

Jung

"Oi! Piss off or I'll smash your fucking face, you son of a bitch!"

"We will shortly be arriving at Laclou station. Laclou, two-minute stop!" announced the ticket inspector.

"Your mum, she sucked me in front of your dad," the aggressive voice resumed.

The train braked suddenly.

There was a screeching noise from the wheels on the rails. I put my fingers in my ears. Even though the train was not full, I had positioned myself in between two carriages since the departure from Bonpomme. Sitting uncomfortably on the floor, shaken throughout the trip, silent, I avoided catching anyone's eye, making myself as small as possible so that nobody would notice me, legs folded against my chest. Insults showered down over my head. They emanated from a big hefty guy in a tracksuit and trainers with a swarthy and scarred face, Oriental eyes and a shaved head. They were intended for a frail boy I thought I saw reflected in the glass of the exit door as I was pulling my suitcase through the crowd that inevitably gathers before a train stops at a station.

"Laclou, two-minute stop!"

A lot of young passengers got off the train, spilling onto the platform of Laclou station, a village I had not known the name of twenty-four hours earlier.

I had been made aware of it on that very morning. Awakened at dawn, my mother had emptied my wardrobe at lightning speed. The suitcase filled with all my old-fashioned and worn clothes, she had thrown a ticket at my face.

"Your train!"

There was in her voice a certain relief and an eagerness that I put down to her being fed up with my presence in her house. I had not left since I had run away from Bonpomme's secondary school. While in previous years I went to summer camps, this summer I did not go anywhere. Knowing that I would not be there after September, she had preferred putting up with me rather than spending part of her widow's pension on a "nobody" like me. The secret hope of a reconciliation, that I had kept alive since the death of my father, quickly vanished. His death did not bring us closer. On the contrary, instead of abusing me, for the past three months she had ignored me, and on the third of September 1987 at eight in the morning I got on a train to Laclou, disillusioned, anxious about what was at the end of that new start, alone and lost. As alone and lost as when I was punished and spent hours moping in my bedroom; as alone and lost as when I arrived at Christ School; as alone and lost as in the garden where even the insects had abandoned me.

Alone and lost since the torrential rains that saw me born, I felt powerless. There had been the ten francs Mr Jadu had given to me but they had only served to violate my privacy. There had been Matthieu, but he had never written to me; Freddy, but he had been imprisoned; Kimpôl, but he lived on the other side of the Channel. And now I had no friends and no bearings, dragging a suitcase whose handle was broken and the zip useless, a suitcase I had to hold in my arms to keep it from opening.

I followed the flow of travellers unsteadily, like an anonymous person treading upon an unknown territory. I left the station head down, one hand on each side of my luggage.

"You're still there, you motherfucker? I told you to clear off!"

I looked up. The frail boy in the train, it was me and my metre sixty-five; the insults I had heard on board, they were intended for me.

"My father," I replied with a delay, "he is—"

A slap sent me to the ground. I dropped my suitcase, which opened. The wind rose. There was a gust and my clothes scattered.

"Your father is what, you son of a bitch?" he roared.

I wiped the blood from my nose.

"He's dead."

Distraught, he made a gesture of exasperation then held out his hand.

"You're too stupid. You could have told me before."

He picked me up, straightened his glasses.

"I took you for someone else," he apologised. "At The Manor, there is an asshole who looks like you and I thought it was him, and without my fucking glasses I can't see well."

"What manor?"

"The Manor, moron! You're going to The Manor, it's obvious. Looking at your clueless mug, you can only go to The Manor... Well, let's not hang around, or there will be no space on the bus. I don't want to waste my time waiting. Follow me."

He pushed his way through a crowd of young people from different backgrounds waiting outside the station, luggage at their feet. Three white minibuses arrived. They reminded me of the one I got in some time ago on the way to Bonny-sur-Geoy.

"And your suitcase, nutcase?" he asked me as the vehicle was starting.

I had forgotten it in the confusion of our meeting.

"What is The Manor?" I asked.

"Are you taking the piss? That's where we're all going. School."

A train ticket with Laclou printed on it, that was all I knew about my destination.

"The Manor of Woe," he told me. "Why are you here?"

"My mother didn't want me anymore."

"Which form are you in?"

"I don't know…"

"You're mental! You've got no more clothes and you don't give a shit. You don't know which form you're in… Do you at least know what your name is?"

Victor and Jung

"This is my third year at The Manor," Jung explained. "As I'm repeating my year, those bastards, they made me come before everyone. Tomorrow I have to see all those idiots, the headmaster, the psychologist, the housemaster, my boarding tutor, teachers and my form tutor. They'll go on with the same crap as usual. Anyway, I don't give a fuck. Will only have to pretend I'm listening and it will be fine…"

Then he was silent. You could hear the engine noise. I looked at Jung discreetly. There was something familiar about his face. It reminded me of Kimpôl. After leaving the village of Laclou, the minibus took a country road and then a narrow path on the left leading to a bridge. We passed through a forest. No one spoke. Apprehension prevailed. I later learned that all those quiet young people, including myself, were new pupils: we would spend the next day getting used to the area and to our respective houses, and the day after, the day before classes resumed, it would be the turn of the others to arrive.

The three minibuses which followed each other came out of the forest, revealing the vast Estate of Woe below. They rushed down the slope, parked by skidding in front of the U-shaped manor and disgorged on a gravelled square their young load originating from the four corners of the world. Boarding tutors scattered them in a dozen houses that were perched at the top of a hundred steps before leaving to look for more trouble that awaited them at Laclou station. To the young with problems, ten- to eighteen-year-old boys, abused, molested, abandoned, asocial, marginal, offenders, The Manor of Woe, an unusual boarding school, unique in the country, was the last opportunity to hang on to a society that had damaged them. To fix them, The Manor of Woe offered vocational training in the hope that once they got their diploma they would start working as soon as possible and would not go off the rails once again. Millers, turners, fitters, mechanics, waiters, cooks, frame-makers, carpenters, gardeners… the skills the world of work needed. There were two restaurants in The Manor. To the left of the large residence, there were classrooms, a joiner's and many other workshops and a garage. Behind the seventeenth-century building, one could see flower gardens and endless cultivated fields, and in front, separated by a river, there were football pitches, basketball and tennis courts, field hockey, and a sports centre that allowed boarders who were only returning home for school holidays time to unwind at the weekend.

"At the Pyramid, where I believe you will stay until you pass your baccalaureate or your vocational diploma, rules are based on respect for each other. The respect of those around you. Your schoolmates. The adults, be they tutors or teachers, they are not here to maintain order but to lend you their full support… Never forget it. Support that you need. You have been through difficult experiences, traumatic for some of you, and you will experience times of doubt, but there will always be someone to listen to you and do everything possible to find a solution. Because there is always a solution. Believe me…"

I was flabbergasted. The priest who spoke, and to whom a boarding tutor was giving a glass of water and an aspirin, I knew him: he was the man who had driven me back home to Bonny-sur-Geoy in his white minibus.

Father Broniel drank from his glass in one go, wetting the top of his thick white beard. His headache persisted but he refused the chair that was brought to him.

"You were told you were worth nothing," he flared up. "You were told life would have been better if you didn't exist. You were told you had no future. Those lies were said again and again until you believed them, until you despised yourself. You lost respect for yourself so you fell on the battlefield. Wounded but not dead. So get back up. You are young. You have your whole life ahead of you. To move forward, you are going to fight. It will not be easy but I believe in you, in your strength of character, in your desire to get through. You will make friends, you will study, you will do sport. I am not asking you to pray. I will pray for you."

Father Broniel gave the audience a paternal glance, and with a step that was meant to be steady, he left the large room furnished with a TV, a table football game, a billiards table, a library, tables and chairs – the main room of the eldest boys' house.

Then a boarding tutor gave us a tour of the Pyramid. The reception, tutors' offices, a screening room, a weights room and a canteen completed the ground floor. Above and on three floors were about a hundred single bedrooms for students preparing for a vocational diploma or a baccalaureate. As one of the fifteen or so young people who were following him in silence, I was allocated a bedroom on the first floor by the tutor.

Just as I walked in, there was a knock on my door. It opened immediately. It was Jung, arms full of clothes, which he threw on my bed. He had helped himself in the school's laundry room.

"With these you'll look less pathetic… Your stuff, did you find it in a second-hand shop or in a bin?"

As I did not react, he chose a pair of jeans, a T-shirt and trainers for me.

"Get changed and come see me when you're ready, my room is next door. And move your arse, it's time to eat…"

After lunch, we sat at a table in the main room of the Pyramid, also called the chill-out room. Table football games were rife. I shared my astonishment with Jung.

"Father Broniel, I'm sure it was him who brought me back home. How is it possible?"

Jung replied that there were inexplicable things that happened. He told me that he, too, a little over two years earlier, had bumped into him outside a nightclub.

"There was an arsehole who was pissing me off. He was showing off. I beat the crap out of him and bouncers threw both of us out. I was so pissed off that I took an iron bar and I was going to beat his arse to death, when Father Broniel stood between us. It was as if he had been warned that I was going to make the biggest mistake of my life. I would have killed that son of a bitch. Two months later, I was at The Manor. I always thought it was all down to my brother…"

He then told me that Father Broniel was the only person he respected at The Manor.

"I heard he was in the war and spent ten years in Africa as a missionary. He must have seen a lot of shit in his life. Did you notice he's not in great shape? Some say he has a rare disease and that he will die soon."

"How old is he?"

"He's going to be sixty."

I changed the subject.

"Your brother, is he here?"

"He was. He left."

"Where is he now?"

"Don't know. He's gone, that's it."

He was starting to get annoyed.

"You don't see him anymore?"

"No I don't!" he said curtly.

I felt the need to talk, the need to know. Jung intrigued me.

"And you, why are you here?"

"You ask too many questions. You've never been taught to shut your mouth?"

Far too much. But the speech of Father Broniel had done me good. "Wounded but not dead." The discussion was perking me up. I insisted. Jung clenched his fist. Thinking he was going to hit me, I instinctively protected my face. The table shook. The table football enthusiasts stopped playing.

"Who asked you, motherfuckers?" Jung said to them.

They resumed their game. We went out to get some fresh air. We skirted around the Pyramid, entering the forest surrounding the Estate of Woe, and walked up a slope. He took a packet of cigarettes from the pocket of his faded jeans.

"You want one?"

The peace pipe. The first puff forced me to sit down. I felt dizzy.

"Why am I here? I have never been asked that question before. Do you really want to know?"

I nodded.

"I bumped my parents off."

"Bumped off?"

"Yeah, I killed them."

Shocked by this revelation, I moved back, trying to get away. Before I could do anything, I found my head clenched between his arm and chest.

"And now that you know, I have to kill you as well," he whispered in an icy tone that sent shivers down my spine.

He grabbed a branch. I wriggled but he was too strong. The branch was held high. I screamed in terror, felt it brushing against my skull then it fell at my feet. The grip loosened. Jung laughed.

"I got you, squirt," he said, going from laughter to tears. "You really thought I was going to kill you. You're such a pussy."

I stood up, confused.

"Stay there! It was a joke. I didn't kill my parents. And I would never hurt you."

He lit up another cigarette and took a long drag, as if to immortalise the moment. Dead leaves quivered. He observed a minute of silence, put on his glasses, and looked around, ensuring that no one was spying on us.

"Come back and sit down, wimp."

Not knowing where to stand, I hesitated.

"Come on, sit down. Sorry if I scared the shit out of you but I couldn't help it... Come here. You're my mate. We're mates, you and me. For life. I got an idea. Let's make a deal..."

He pulled out a Swiss army knife and handed it to me after making an incision in his wrist. I did the same. We then made a blood oath. I resumed my questions.

"Why are you at The Manor?"

"I had no other place to go. Since I was eight, I've ran away from nine host families. Some believed I was their son. Some others believed I was their stooge. In the last family I fucked their daughter. She was so hot. A proper slut. But then she played the innocent. I couldn't believe it. They got rid of me straight away."

Rather than reporting to the juvenile court judge's summons, like the previous eight times, he wandered around, and a few hours later, he went to a nightclub. It was the night he met Father Broniel.

"Where are you from?" I asked.

"From an orphanage."

Jung was born in North Korea.

"What happened to your parents?"

He was not laughing anymore. He tried to hide his sorrow but I saw a tear running down his face.

His parents were opponents of his native country's regime. Reported by a neighbour, the police had tried everything to make them talk: they wanted names. He did not understand; he was seven. Broken fingers, burnt feet, flesh opened, they had been tortured before his eyes in his childhood shack. Then they were shot in the head.

"Before leaving, they did this to me," he continued, putting his finger on a long scar that ran from his torso down to his groin. "And that…"

He touched the scar across his face.

"But I was lucky. They thought I was dead and they left."

I put my hand on his shoulder. I realised that my suffering was nothing compared to his.

"And your brother, where was he?"

"He was at the factory."

"At the factory? How old was he?"

"In my country it's not like here. Over there, you work from a young age. He was ten… When he returned home, I thought it was the police coming back. I played dead. And something weird happened. I saw my brother and his double. I know you're not going to believe me but it's the truth. When I tell you that there are things you can't explain… Two people, but the same two."

Half unconscious, he had witnessed the splitting of his brother. And while one was crying about his parents, the other one was taking care of his younger brother's injuries.

Jung felt drained. I understood he no longer had the strength to speak. We returned to the Pyramid.

He never talked to me again about the events that marked his childhood. Having said too much for his liking, he avoided me, to the extent that during the first days of school I felt betrayed. We had made a pact he did not respect. So I would sit at the back of the classroom, silent. I would not listen to the lessons, and then after school I would shut myself away in my bedroom, doubting my ability to adapt to the boarding life in this huge school where nearly six hundred boys lived together in a dozen small buildings. Their problems did not interest me. Father Broniel's invigorating speech already seemed far away. The idea of fighting for three years to get a baccalaureate seemed senseless. It seemed even more absurd when I learned that Jung had run away.

10

Anatole

At the news of his disappearance, I left the classroom in a fury. I rushed up the hundred steps leading to the Pyramid and entered the chill-out room. Chairs, video recorder, television, tables, table football, they all flew around me. I broke everything I could. When the housemaster, protected with a shield, a remnant of a previous riot squad career, finally managed to remove the armchair blocking the entrance of the room, he skilfully avoided the salvo of pool balls I fired at him. When I had no more ammunition, I was overpowered by the housemaster helped by three boarding tutors. The damage had been done. The chill-out room looked like a battlefield. I had lost my nerves. I was sent to the school psychologist's office.

"Problems can't be resolved with violence," said the man sitting opposite me on the other side of the desk. "Tell me what is happening."

"I didn't ask to be here," I cried. "Screw you."

My file was on the table. I grabbed it and threw it in his face. He bent down to pick up my scattered life.

"Everything is in there. You want me to read it to you?"

"But you, what do you have to say?"

As I did not answer, he put a white sheet on the table and gave me a pencil.

"Draw here what you feel."

"What's the point?"

"To know you better. You haven't written what is in your file. The drawing, it's you who is going to do it. Draw what you want."

"And you think that by looking at my drawing, you're going to understand who I am? You really think I'm going to change and I'll get my baccalaureate? You're missing the point. You're like the others."

"What are the others like?"

"They don't care about me."

"Who are the others?"

"The others, it's all those who have let me down and didn't lift a finger when I wasn't all right. My mother who never loved me, my father who beat me, people in my village who knew what was going on in my home, teachers who also knew. Even those I thought were my friends."

"Are you referring to your friend Jung?"

Matthieu, Freddy, Kimpôl and now Jung. New-found friendships which went up in smoke.

"Life has no interest to me," I blurted out, disillusioned. "I don't know what the hell I'm doing in this world and I don't need help."

The psychologist looked at me with his square eyes.

"You're mistaken. You need support and you will come to see me regularly. We'll not let you down. At The Manor, hundreds of young people made it and there is no reason you'll not follow the same path… This drawing, you'll do it at your own pace. But I'd like to see it at some point."

There was a knock at the door. He pointed to the exit. A queue had formed in the hallway. Boys bearing the marks of the past on their faces were waiting for their turn.

When I arrived at the end of the miserable queue, time had passed. Christmas holidays were about to start. I felt apprehensive about seeing my mother again. But that did not happen. She had decided otherwise.

I looked at the Estate emptying of most of its students, who squeezed onto the white minibuses. Should I envy them or be happy to be among the half-dozen boarders who would remain at the Pyramid during the holidays?

I had a peaceful Christmas, and at Easter I also stayed at The Manor but this time without misgivings. I only returned to Bonny-sur-Geoy in June 1988, nine months after my hasty departure.

I found my mother in a sorry state. She looked ten years older, had not changed clothes for a long time and smelled like piss. The house had become a slum. There was mouldy food on plates scattered in every room. A centimetre of dirt covered the floor. The sheets of her bed were yellowish. As for the garden, it was full of weeds. I immediately set to the task. I cleaned the house from top to bottom. The sight and the unbearable smell of the toilet made me vomit. Like a zombie, my mother would wander and then sit on the floor, empty eyes, mind elsewhere. To the sound of my voice, she would raise her head, staring at me, nod and then stand up again, pacing the living room up and down before going back upstairs and shutting herself up in her bedroom. On Sundays she did not go to Mass anymore, and when I went for a walk in the village, I heard people whispering "It's the madwoman's son". I visited Father Moino, who promised to come to see her regularly, and in early September I took the train back to Laclou.

I had done just enough to go into the second year of my baccalaureate but now I had to get down to work. On the menu for the next two years was a technological baccalaureate in electrical engineering. My classmates had previously completed technical training, but for me, technology did not mean anything.

"Put your metal piece in the vice, tighten it, bring the cutter closer and work your piece. Watch out for the chips. Victor, put your protective go…"

"Too easy," I told myself. My milling machine was the first one to hum. Even though I had no idea of the final result and felt I was controlled by the machine, I was, without a doubt, making something, machining the material with all my spirit, convincing myself that I was acting like a proper milling machine operator. This thought was as ridiculous as it was dangerous. I screamed in pain, my face on fire, blinded by the heat of the chips.

"Your protective goggles, Victor!"

Bloody chips! As if that was not enough, the rotary motion made the loose piece of metal come out of the vice. I instinctively reached out. The burning hot piece of metal landed in the palm of my hand. I shrieked. I bumped my head against the machine tool. I yelled. The teacher pressed the emergency stop button.

Defeated by the machine on my first attempt!

From then on, to my lack of interest was grafted an aversion for machine tools as well as for everything related to the world of automation and manual work. Electrical engineering lessons did not carry as many dangers but my electrical connection work and my pasting of electronic components did not let the current go through or switch on the multicoloured LEDs. As for technical drawing, in the same way as I refused to represent what I felt inside me – the psychologist was still waiting for my drawing – I was unable to represent what I saw in space, be it a top, a bottom or a side view. The promising industry that had been presented to us was not for me.

"Help yourself and success will follow. You're not stupid. You can manage."

These words came from Anatole, my class boarding tutor.

"You all say the same thing," I replied. "You all say that we can manage. So easy to say. I don't understand anything about mechanics, electricity, electronics. How do you want me to manage?"

"If you could eventually get to work instead of bumming around in class, you'd see it more clearly and results would follow."

But nothing got into my head, and I was feeling quite depressed in my bedroom at the beginning of November 1988 when someone gently knocked on my door.

I thought I would faint at the sight of the haggard boy who gave me a hug. Jung, in person and with a bag full of clothes.

"This is for you, my friend. So you won't look like a tramp anymore."

I did not believe it.

"Where were you?"

"I screwed up. But I haven't forgotten you, my friend."

He took out two beers from the bag.

"Let's toast!"

It was my first sip of alcohol. He drank his beer in one go. I forgave him for his betrayal. He spoke quickly: "I can't hang around. I came through the forest and I have the cops on my tail. I tracked down my brother, and when you're finished here, you must meet me in London. He lives there. I wrote the address on that piece of paper. Don't lose it, nutcase. I have to clear off. See you in two years."

And as fast as he had appeared, he disappeared. Five minutes later, a siren sounded from outside the Pyramid. It was followed by a racket on the stairs. Then a violent blow on the door. Hinges and screws flew in the air. The door fell, knocked down. A dozen cowboys rushed into my bedroom with the housemaster behind them.

"Where is he?" roared the latter, drenched in sweat while the men with hats, side by side, were inspecting every corner of the room.

"Who?"

"Don't make fun of me. You know who I'm talking about. Your friend Jung. We know he came. Well! Look..." He pointed to the travel bag and the two beers.

"Send some men into the forest. The suspect fled the scene," the sheriff said into his walkie-talkie.

He kept one of his men with him and sent half of his troops in pursuit of Jung while the others cordoned off the house.

"Search him!" he ordered.

The address was in my pocket. I wadded it into a ball and ate it without being seen.

The voice of the Pyramid's housemaster blasted: "Your friend has robbed the clothes shop in Laclou. It is in your best interests to tell us what you know if you don't want to be accused of complicity. You have already been in trouble with the law. It would be a shame if it happens again."

"What did he do, this one?" asked the sheriff while feeling the star of his authority.

"He was involved in the Christ School case."

The sheriff put his hand on the holster of his gun, ready to draw at the slightest dirty trick.

"He is neither armed nor dangerous," said a soft voice from the hallway. "And until proven otherwise, he is innocent." It was Anatole. "A call for you Jean-Paul!" he added.

"It can wait," retorted the portly and overzealous housemaster.

"It is an urgent call."

The search was unsuccessful. The remaining men of the Far West law enforcement left with the bag of clothes. Jean-Paul followed suit. I hoped they would not catch Jung.

"What a mess!" exclaimed Anatole.

"I don't get it," I replied. "The door wasn't locked."

"Like in the movies," he sighed... "Well, let's get back to work now, Victor. The show is over. Should I remind you that mock exams are starting tomorrow?"

My door was repaired. Then, led by Anatole, I began to revise. He stood by my side for the rest of the school year, a year marked by the death of Father Broniel, who passed away in February 1989. Was it purely coincidental or did I get Divine help? The charges of complicity in the murder of Augustin le Fonbou were withdrawn shortly after. The sessions with the psychologist became less frequent. I would visit him only once a month. Despite having numerous arguments with everyone, I managed to get noticed without breaking anything. It happened at the annual Manor of Woe cross-country which took place in April. The year before, I had walked all the way and had been the very last to cross the finishing line. This time I put all my aggression into the race and won it. Spurred on by the sports teacher, I lived and breathed through, and for, sport. Every day, straight after school, I would rush to my bedroom, put on shorts, shirt, shoes, and off I would go. My progress was dazzling and success followed. A few races won, county champion, inter-counties runner-up. The newspapers talked about me once again. But spoke well of me. My picture in the centre of the sports page. I was proud. I was training to the point of making myself sick. Running became my priority.

"You all right, Marathon Man?"

Marathon Man... Far more heart-warming than Skeletor...

"Coming for a run?"

"I'm... I'm... I'm co... co... coming!" replied Fabrice, a shy boy who stuttered. Like each of us, he had had problems. We never talked about them. It was an unwritten rule at The Manor.

He was one of the orphans from the Bordeaux region. There were eight in my class, the final year of my baccalaureate, and they had a strong sense of solidarity. I had learned it the hard way.

"You are all idiots!" I had shouted out, upset, after one of them had told me to stop disrupting the lessons.

They banned me from their circle for two long weeks. Not a word was addressed to me and they stuck to their word. The incident closed, they became my best friends and it is with them that I got drunk for the first time.

Although drinks with unpredictable effects were not allowed within the school premises, they would find a way to bring alcohol in. On a Saturday night, they decided to have fun. I was invited to the party. Music, noise, alcohol and smoking: what could be more normal when boys decide to put studies aside? That night, it took three of them to put me to bed. The next morning, waking up had been hard and it was with difficulty that I ran into the forest, in which, under normal circumstances, I would fill my lungs with pure country air while flying like a rocket through the trees. With stitches, and breathless, I finally had to sit behind the Pyramid, on the very spot where I had made a blood oath with Jung. I was supposed to meet him after taking my baccalaureate but our reunion was in jeopardy. I had swallowed the address he had given to me and London seemed far, far away, out of reach.

"Get up Victor! It's eight thirty. Your classmates are already in class. Maybe it's about time you got your act together if you want to pass your exam. You certainly won't succeed by staying in bed. It's all very well to run, but it's the third time this week I've had to come to wake you up and I'm not going to keep on doing that until the exams!"

"All right… getting up!"

Anatole went out of my bedroom… and I fell back into the land of Nod.

Midday… Damn it! I jumped out of bed. I had to find a good excuse.

I had to go into the housemaster's office. Since the police had raided the Pyramid, he had barely spoken to me.

"I didn't go to class…"

"And yet a tutor did come to wake you up…"

"I'm sorry, but I couldn't get up. Last night, I had a terrible nightmare. I didn't sleep all night and when Anatole came in, I thought I was dreaming."

He sighed.

"OK, go and have your lunch…"

My story made the whole table laugh.

"You're such a clown, Victor!"

"So what! I slept well and I'm fit to study…"

"Do you think you're going to study? No way! You're going to sleep in class. As usual. Look... Anatole is coming to talk to you..."

"You stayed in bed this morning, you lazy boy! You really need to sort your act out," he snapped at me. "I'll come to see you tonight. We must talk about the exams."

In the evening, the sound of footsteps brought me out of my dreams.

"Now listen, Victor. It is out of the question that I can look after you next year. You will get your baccalaureate this year. If you find some subjects difficult, I can help you. You're definitely not stupid. If you at least made an effort..."

"Don't worry," I replied calmly. "It seems like I'm not doing anything, but it's not true."

"Don't take the piss out of me! Your marks are not great. Your application in class is dreadful. And you dare to claim you do enough... You've got one more term, just one."

That evening, things fell into place.

This baccalaureate, I wanted to get it so badly that I began to swot like never before. There would not be a single evening when I would be on my own. I would sail along bedrooms, ready to catch any information, any explanation. An open door: I would be inside the bedroom in no time. No subjects overlooked. All the best students put to the test. I was also attending lessons diligently. Last in the class, any noise during lessons would make me angry.

"Shut up! I would like to listen..."

"Calm down..."

"You calm down, both of you!" thundered the old man whose job was to teach us technical drawing. He grabbed a piece of chalk, broke it in two and threw one half in our direction. A chain smoker, he put the other half in his mouth and puffed on it.

"Anyway," said the idiot sitting behind me, "you'll speak when you get your baccalaureate, not before..."

The baccalaureate, always the baccalaureate, and yet again the baccalaureate... As I was not in a position to respond, I stayed quiet.

And the nearer the exams drew, the more the tension mounted. I was planning to get an average mark of ten out of twenty, no more, no less, coming up with a predicted mark for each subject: mathematics, physics, English and French were to make up for technical drawing, mechanical engineering and automation.

Every minute was precious; every idea found, one more point gained; every word, a better appreciation from examiners. Time was running out. The automation paper: the program worked, the mechanical arm did what it was supposed to do. Technical drawing: the miracle; I drew, traced, erased. I drew a screw from all possible angles. I was exulting… But still, doubt remained. A stressful eve of the results. We were in a café in Laclou. Laughs were not genuine. We were all tense. Dodgy jokes. The big day. It was the morning. It was sunny. Anatole knew. His lips were moving. I heard strange, incomprehensible, unbelievable words. No. I could not believe it. Me, a failure…

"It's not true!"

"I'm telling you. Go downstairs."

I went down the stairs six by six.

"Bravo, Victor! Congratulations!"

The housemaster congratulated me, shaking my hand, no hard feelings. I still could not believe it. Did something turn my luck around? I went back up quickly. I wanted to be on my own. I wanted to savour my victory. Upstairs, I erupted with joy. I jumped wildly. I grabbed a bottle of whisky. I drank from the bottle, non-stop. My head spun. I felt sick.

11

Mr Pinson

I opened my eyes painfully. It was daylight. I was in my bedroom. At home. In Bonny-sur-Geoy. I had a headache, a furred tongue and the feeling I should have got up earlier. My foot stumbled against a glass bottle. I went down the stairs carefully.

I cast a glance at the calendar hanging on the kitchen wall. "January 1" announced the long-neglected tear-off calendar with irony. On the table there was a letter.

"Fuck!" I shouted. "My appointment!"

I rushed to the living room, checked the date of my interview against the date indicated by the computer. March 17, 1997. They matched. My appointment was at half past eleven and it was... quarter past twelve. I tried to redeem myself by contacting the Bonpomme employment agency.

"You had been warned that if you didn't turn up you wouldn't be given another chance. I'm sorry but this is not the first time you put us in this situation. We can't do anything for you anymore... There is a new agency that has just opened in Bonpomme. Try your luck with them."

I went there the next day. I recognised the recruiting officer of the new temporary work agency. I had seen him one day arm in arm with Geneviève, the headmaster's daughter. He browsed through my CV, looking sorry.

"You are right. We're looking for technical salesmen, but with at least one year's experience in sales. You don't have any diploma and you don't have any experience. So I can't offer you anything in this field. However, I can see on your CV that you have worked on production lines. We always need semi-skilled workers…"

*

Going to bed at dawn after a night tightening strings around piles of newspapers, to wake up, late afternoon, depressed; starting at 2pm to fill the day and part of the night with pathetic tasks; getting up at half past four in the morning after a sleepless night to clock in just before six o'clock feeling like shit, disgusted by the cigarette smoked on the way to the factory: I had had enough. Weary from three years of three-shift assembly-line work, dejected, I had broken down. The monotony of the work, the deathly pale faces of the employees and the dullness of my life got the better of me and one morning I had thrown in the towel.

*

"We are also looking for electricians."

*

Leaving on Monday morning to return on Sunday evening a fortnight later; housed with strangers in crummy hotels, cockroaches under the sheets; thirteen hours a day on building sites where it was cold; told off all day long because the connecting wires were not long enough or because the hole in the ceiling from where they were supposed to come out was not big enough: I did not last long.

After working in production lines and on construction sites, I had unplugged my digital alarm clock, bought a TV and joined, with relief, the two million unemployed.

*

"If only you had passed your baccalaureate, maybe I could have found a way…"

If I had passed my baccalaureate… And to think that back then I firmly believed I would. I had even chosen a career. After getting my diploma, I was planning to go on a two-year course and learn marketing. A promising future. Selling, buying. A guaranteed job. A good salary.

"By how many points did you fail?"

"Sorry?"

"By how many points did you fail your baccalaureate?"

"I didn't take it."

*

Back in May 1990, shortly before the exams, Father Moino got in touch with me. As he did every morning, he had visited my mother. As there was no answer at the door, he entered. She had locked herself in her bedroom.

"She wants to see you, Victor. You must come or she may do something irredeemable."

He was panicking and he felt powerless. He had to promise her he would not contact anyone else but me. If he dared to call the fire department or the police, she had sworn she would end her life. I took the first train to Bonny-sur-Geoy and never returned to The Manor.

My baccalaureate, I would take it again and again, but only in my dreams.

*

"How is Geneviève?" I asked.

"How do you know my wife?"

"We were in the same class at school."

He put a hand on his belly.

"She's fine. She's pregnant."

"And Mr Pinson?"

"He can't wait for the birth of his grandson… or granddaughter."

Then he began to think about a solution. One could hear the monotonous voice of his colleague in talks with a jobless hyper-graduate.

"Regarding this technical sales job," he murmured to me, "I see only one solution."

"Well…?"

"Rewrite your CV," he whispered. "Expand it and come back to see me this afternoon. But it must stay between us. I don't want to get into trouble."

A helping hand of fate. That is what I needed. I thanked him, left the agency and returned to Bonny-sur-Geoy on my bike. I updated my CV.

I added an *s* to the word *diploma,* a technological baccalaureate in electrical engineering and an HND in marketing after my pathetic BEPC. In the *Professional Experience* section, I replaced the embarrassing list of miserable jobs and my period of unemployment with four years in sales, *from February 15, 1993 to February 21, 1997*. The name of the company, its business and location still needed to be added.

"May I speak to Anatole, the boarding tutor from the Pyramid. I am a former pupil of The Manor."

"Please hold the line…"

"Hello…"

Anatole's serene voice.

"Anatole, I need a big favour."

I told him my plan.

"It's not a joke, is it… Give me your number. I'll call you in a few minutes."

My phone rang. Matille-Chinou Company, a machine tool supplier based in Laclou.

"We send our young people there to do their work experience. The boss is called Mr Saifreur. It might be useful to know it in case you're asked."

"Thanks, Anatole. I haven't got much time. We'll keep in touch."

Once my CV was completed and printed, I took it to the agency. And landed the job. One day of training and then I would sell printers. Without any knowledge of the subject, I started studying my own printer, which bored me to death. I turned the TV on.

12

Father Moino

Wednesday, March 26, 1997

6:00: The alarm rang. One arm stretched out, turned the alarm clock off; there was an imperceptible movement of the eyelids.

6:15: It rang again. The same arm, the right, the same movement.

6:30: The radio alarm clock was disconnected. Snore. Outside, behind the curtains, the sun was rising.

Undefined time: From a lying position, the upper body stood up straight. Eyes opened. The head turned towards the digital device. It did not tell the time. Action stations. The eyes, the bed, the curtains were opened.

In boxer shorts and shirtless, I went down the stairs as fast as I could. What time was it? My training day was to begin at half past eight. Could not find my watch. The computer did not turn on. I called the speaking clock.

"…and twenty-eight seconds… It is seven, fifty-nine and…"

I was in trouble. Had to be on-site in thirty minutes. Would have my breakfast on the way, on my bike. First, I called my employer. Had to find an excuse.

"I'm sorry. I have a punctured tyre. I'll be late. I'm sorry."

The shower postponed to a later date. Water on my face. Too-close shaving. Top lip cut. I was bleeding. A plaster over it. The aftershave slipped for no reason from my hands. The cream spread on the floor, on my feet. My suit. My only suit which I had not worn for years. I had promised myself to iron it. No time to do it now. My trousers were creased. The jacket would hide the shirt, which had not been ironed either. The tie. Where was the fucking tie? A bow tie would do. Better than nothing. I was dressed, I was washed... My perfume. I returned to the bathroom. Grabbed it, forgetting there was cream on the floor. I slipped, held myself back on the sink, the bottle fell, exploded. My feet and now my socks smelled clean. I was ready. No. Almost forgot my breakfast. Leftover baguette from the day before yesterday. When I worked, I was eating well. Since I had no job, I would eat whatever I found. The bread was stale. Too late for coffee. Lack of organisation. I was not used to it anymore. It had been a year since I last worked, received unemployment benefit and let myself go.

Shit... The folder!

"Fill in the form," Mr Pinson's son-in-law had told me.

I had filled it in.

"Bring the folder the agency has given you," my future boss had reminded me a few minutes earlier.

And he was not fooling around.

I searched my pockets. My keys... They were in my jacket hanging on the coat rack behind the door. A door I had just slammed. I would do without the folder. Would find a reason on the way. My bike. I sat on the saddle, started pedalling. A wheel's turn. I did not go further. I did have a punctured tyre. Hitch-hiking. The building of the printing company.

The secretary looked up and down at the young man who had just entered. Tousled hair, sleep around the eyes, a plaster on the upper lip, dried spots of blood – she counted seven of them – a strange diagonal bow tie, a jacket with a torn pocket handkerchief, a shirt hanging over a shapeless pair of trousers, old and unpolished shoes, a sickening smell of cologne…

"Looking for something?" she asked, holding her nose.

"I'm sorry I'm late. I had a transport problem. It's because of my bike."

"Are you Victor Vimord?" she asked with surprise. "Are you the new recruit? Sit over there. I'll see if Mister De Lancre is available."

I sat on the sofa, feeling pangs of hunger.

"He is here," I heard the secretary say. "Yes… I'll ask him to wait… His file… Very well, Mister De Lancre… Yes, Mister De Lancre…"

She put down the handset.

"Mister De Lancre is busy. Did you bring your file?"

She pressed the intercom button once again.

"He doesn't have his file… Yes, I know… Yes, two hours late… Very well, Mister De Lancre… And I'll call back the agency… I will, Mister De Lancre. I will…"

She showed me the door.

"You may leave now."

"I can come back this afternoon. It's just that I left my house without my keys and my file was…"

She showed me the door again. I was disappointed. I returned home. The answering machine was blinking. There were two messages. The first one struck me off the list of the employment agency. I erased it. The trembling voice on the second message took me aback.

"Victor? I hope this is the right number. My name is Raymond, Raymond Puttere. I am your uncle. Could you contact me on 20 12 31 13 and ask for room number four? It is urgent."

The name brought me back to May 1990, seven years earlier.

*

I had left The Manor of Woe. Father Moino was waiting for me on the platform of Bonpomme's train station.

"We have to hurry. Your mother is not doing well at all. I fear she may do something irredeemable. She is threatening to take her life."

We climbed the stairs.

"Yvette, I am with Victor," said Father Moino.

We heard the sound of bottles clinking.

"Yvette, your son is here."

"I want to see Raymond!" she bellowed in a drunken voice. "Or I will slit my throat."

"Victor is here," repeated Father Moino.

"I'm not crazy. In the village they say I'm crazy. I want to see Raymond. He knows I'm not crazy."

I put my ear against the door.

"Mum, it's me."

"Who is it?"

"It's me, Victor."

"Victor? Don't know any Victor. Where is Raymond?"

I looked at Father Moino.

"Mum, who is Raymond?"

"Everybody knows who Raymond is. My mother she loves her Raymond. I'm going to drink to Raymond's health and to my mother and to all my brothers and sisters."

A long gurgling, a silence and then a sound of breaking glass. I jumped. Worried, Father Moino came close to the door.

"Yvette, is everything all right?"

She was crying.

"Mum, open the door!" I begged her. "Open the door. You wanted to see me, I'm here. Talk to me."

She stopped crying.

"Victor?"

She then started to laugh, an evil laughter that sent shivers down my spine.

"I'm crazy, aren't I? You think I'm crazy. Ask Raymond if I'm crazy. He knows. He knows everything."

"What does he know, Mum?"

"Stop calling me Mum. I'm not your mother. I have no children. It's not me, your mother."

I turned to Father Moino.

"She is raving," he assured me.

"I heard you, Father. I'm not crazy. He also knows I'm not his mother. My baby died in my womb. They wanted to have me believe a lie. Ask Raymond. He knows the truth. My baby died. He's in my womb."

Despite the absurdity of her words, I subconsciously believed what she said. As she became unintelligible, I brought up the idea of calling the fire brigade. My mother threw herself against the door.

"You'll have my death on your conscience if you do that. I swear on my life I'll kill myself."

"What do you want me to do? I'm sick of your bullshit," I said, rising up. "You want me to call Raymond? OK, I'll do it. Give me his number."

She opened a bottle of wine.

"Your father knows it."

"My father is dead. Don't you remember?"

"I'm not crazy, worthless son. It's your fault he died. If you weren't born he'd be alive."

"I thought I wasn't your son."

"You're nothing to me. You're an accident. I didn't want you. You're not my son. Ghislaine is dead because of you. You're the devil. You bring bad luck. You—"

I cut short the discussion.

"Give me the number or I'll call the fire brigade."

She had carved it with a knife on the wooden kitchen table. I dialled the number. Made quickly aware of the situation, Raymond

Puttere refused to come to Bonny-sur-Geoy. When the stillborn baby my mother talked about was mentioned, he hung up.

Behind the bedroom door, the reaction was swift. My mother knocked back the bottle in one go. We heard the sound of broken glass; a rattle; a body falling. Then silence.

Called in, firemen smashed the door. The face of my mother was bathed in a pool of blood, the throat cut open. I fainted.

*

So years of uncertainty and nightmares began. Tormented by guilt at the death of these two people who I was not even sure had been my parents, I fell asleep deep into the night. Eyes barely closed, I felt evil presences in my bedroom; my breathing became more difficult; I choked; these presences came closer and closer to my bed. I tried to speak: words would not come out. I tried to open my eyes: I could not see. I tried to get up: my body was numb. Presences touched my bed. I was scared. So scared I drew deep down within myself to shake myself up. A scream in the night. Mine. Presences vanished. I lit the lamp. I was sweating. Then I could not find sleep again.

On other nights I would see myself fall into an abyss. A vertiginous fall. Nothing to grab hold of. I was suffocating. I begged for help. I groaned, alone, sinking into a black hole.

One night I heard the grating voice of my mother.

"I'm not your mother. You have no parents. You're an accident. You shouldn't have been born and you will pay for it. You're going to regret being born. You're going to regret it all your bloody life."

I replied I had not done anything wrong.

"This is all your fault, evil child. I curse you. Your life will turn into hell. You're a murderer. You've killed your parents, you've killed Ghislaine and you are the one who's killed Augustin. Murderer! You won't get away with it."

She stood straight, with no neck, Augustin's head on her shoulders, pointing to her own head lying on the floor next to her husband's dismembered body, which an old woman with a purplish-blue face, flayed forehead and hands, was attempting to put back together.

"If you hadn't been born, we would all be alive. Ask Raymond. He knows everything."

A man appeared.

"Let's say I'm your uncle."

As I tried to move towards him, I slipped, fell flat on my face in red water amid scattered limbs floating above the floor.

"Call for help," I cried.

Raymond questioned me.

"One plus one equals…"

"One," I replied.

"Wrong answer," stated Raymond. "If you had been more diligent in class, I could have helped you."

"But that's what I learned in class. One plus one equals one. The current flows."

"And did you pass your so-called baccalaureate?"

"No, my mother didn't want me to get it."

"And a liar with that," my mother roared. "I'm going to cut out your tongue. You will pay for…"

Nightmares haunted my nights for months. As I fell asleep at sunrise and woke up in the afternoon, I skipped meals regularly, losing weight. I did not leave my house, since I was convinced I was paying for wrongdoings I had committed and which, even if I could not identify them, did not give me the right to live normally. A sinner, a nobody: that was who I was.

"A young man who has suffered a lot but shouldn't let himself go!" was the response from Father Moino. I survived thanks to his visits and to the mission he had set his heart on to getting me back on my feet. After taking care of my mother, he looked after me.

My factory and building site jobs, my time of unemployment, my removal from employment agencies and finally the telephone call from that uncle followed.

*

I listened again to the recording, sprawled on the couch. What could be so urgent for this uncle to leave me a message? He had not come for the funeral of his sister and in twenty-five years had not bothered to take an interest in his nephew even once. I decided to call him. He spoke of an inheritance from an aunt called Josiane and asked me to join him.

As nothing was keeping me in Bonny-sur-Geoy, I packed my bags in the evening and then started searching for information about people in Northern France. I had heard they had their own way of speaking. I resolved the computer breakdown by reinserting the plug which was disconnected and I logged on to the internet. I found a glossary of the language spoken in some parts of Northern France, articles on miners and regional recipes.

The next day I would go to Lamheur, the village where my mother was born, a stronghold of the Puttere family, with the firm intention of not leaving until I knew what truth my mother had spoken about before killing herself.

13

Erik

Halemur, situated about ten kilometres from Lamheur.

"WELCOME TO THE STICKS, VICTOR"

The banner stretched from one end to the other of the platform of Halemur station, which was flooded with people. Men, women, boys and girls held me in their arms. Camera flashes made travellers who got off the train turn around. My name was chanted over and over, my cheeks were kissed passionately and my hair was fondled with love. Driven by curiosity, the magazine *Stars of Today* in her hand, an onlooker came nearer to the family circle. Thinking she was a cousin, I let her kiss me, which made the Putteres laugh. Not long after, they were fighting over my bag, a scene filmed by a cameraman sent by the local television company. They lifted me and I left the station on the shoulders of the fifty or so uncles, aunts and cousins. They carried me in triumph to a bus they had booked to pick me up then put me down inside the vehicle. On board, the good-natured mood turned to a frenzy. They were now fighting to be seated as close to me as possible so they had to draw straws to choose a driver – the unlucky one, in tears, resigned himself to taking the wheel – and for the best seats. The luckiest ones sat beside, in front and behind me.

"Bah 'eck 'ow cumly 'e is!"

"'Ow smart 'e is!"

"'E will cum t'ouse."

"Nooa, ta mine fust."

"Talk to him in French. 'E doesn't understan' owt, t' poor thin. Thou can tell."

Overwhelmed with happiness for the interest they had shown in me, as strange as it was since I did not know these people, I smiled foolishly. I barely understood them.

The arrival in Lamheur went from chaos to riot, each family member wanting to take me to their home first. The eldest raised his cane. In an authoritarian tone, Raymond demanded peace and quiet.

"Orl o' yuz, nip on back 'ooam. Ah need ta spek wi' ower nephew."

They scattered in the village, grumbling, while I followed Raymond into his brick house. His wife was in the kitchen. During the meal, the old lady did not open her mouth. As a submissive woman, a gesture from Raymond and she would bring the dishes out. Oxtail verrines, tarte Tatin with caramelised endive, crème brûlée with chicory, all of this washed down with Mort Subite limbic beer: we had a feast. A full plate served: Raymond would throw himself on it, head first, making noises while stuffing himself with his dirty paws. Food stuck on his chin: he would wipe it with his sleeve. He burped after every bottle of beer he drank down, and farted loudly. From time to time, he raised his muzzle to grunt things I did not understand. Then, unexpectedly, he left the table and returned from his garden with a truffle in his muddy mouth.

"My mother also loved her garden," I said.

My comment made him feel uncomfortable.

"Ah doon't want t'urt thee," he replied, "burt thee mutheur, shi wor sick. Even wuss, shi b'trayed uss. Shi is t'un whoa dint want ta see uss anymooar."

"Yet you were the one she wanted to talk to before her death."

"Ah kna. Burrah doon't understan' wha. We 'ed nowt ta seh ta apiece o'tha. T' past is int' past. We dooant tak abaht it."

After a coffee drunk with a straw, I went to another house. The following three days I had my breakfast, lunch and dinner at a different family member's home. They lavished me with attention, gifts and envelopes containing money. From feast to feast, I began to doubt the innocence of their generosity. They were bribing me but I did not know for what purpose. As soon as I mentioned my mother, there was a silence and I would be sent wandering with my youngest cousins who did not seem to be aware of family stories buried for years.

"We dint kna tha yer mam 'n wor deed, poor thin. Did thee tell theur abaht auntie Josiane?"

Aunt Josiane, my eldest aunt, had recently died. No mention had been made about her until now. The widow of a wealthy banker, without direct descendants, she had a fortune to share between her brothers and sisters. The sudden interest of the Puttere family in a nephew they had never cared about had an explanation. "It is urgent," Raymond had told me on the phone. As my mother was no longer living, I was one of the heirs. Without my signature, the inheritance could not be given out. That was my opportunity to worm the truth out of Raymond and the rest of the family. I would not sign until they answered my questions. They had made me come to the middle of nowhere for money. With the money lying dormant in the bank, people's tongues loosened.

Raymond had not lifted a finger for his sister because "'E could nae stand t'lass."

Was she crazy?

Was she born crazy? One is not born crazy.

Which event had traumatised her? No one answered. They were afraid of Raymond.

"Then I won't sign."

I demanded the truth. Otherwise the gifts and the two-hundred-franc notes would have been an investment at a loss.

Raymond was the one to be accused. It was his responsibility to spill the beans.

Now he was defending himself from any involvement. It was not him. He had done nothing. Yes, she was pregnant when she was a teenager.

Who was the father? Someone local. According to the rumours, it was the mayor of Lamheur. The matter had been hushed up.

And the mayor, where was he now? Six feet under.

"Can thee sign now?"

The notary handed me a letter. Then he followed my aunt's last wishes, who had asked that I read it right away. She had also forbidden the presence of her brothers and sisters in the office. So they were outside, waiting for the good news which would make them so rich that they would not have to worry about work anymore. They knew about Josiane's stupendous wealth but were unaware of that letter. I began reading it. It had been written by hand and was addressed to the son of Yvette Puttere.

Victor,

Your mother has been through a lot in her life. We, her brothers and sisters, are partly responsible for it. As she was the youngest, my mother, your grandmother, would mollycoddle her. I wasn't the last one to complain about it, and to get even with her for enjoying preferential treatment, we were horrible to her. I hope that up above she has forgiven me for my jealousy and that you will also forgive me.

What I'm going to tell you will not fill you with any joy but I can't take an unpunished crime with me, a crime which has left its mark on your mother forever. Yvette was a timid and wild teenager. She was afraid of everything, but even more of Raymond. At the time he always had control over all of us, and your mother, being the youngest and most fragile, was even more at his mercy. I feel guilty for not establishing the truth in my lifetime. I have no doubt that Raymond's problems with the law were concealed from you. He was accused of the sexual abuse of minors but was never convicted for lack of evidence. I am convinced he wasn't as innocent as he claimed to be in the rape of your mother.

Before following your father, she left me a letter making me promise it would be opened after her death. I have entrusted Mr Fidaile with it.

I've made arrangements for you to receive my inheritance in its entirety. Raymond won't get a penny. I have also disinherited my other brothers and sisters, who deserve nothing from me. They were all as cowardly as I was.

J. Puttere.

Mr Fidaile gave me an aged envelope. I pulled out a piece of paper on which I recognised my mother's misspellings and rough handwriting:

Raymond rayped me. Soree my son four herting you. Its not my faut.

Everything was now clear in my head. My mother had never liked me because of her brother. My life had been cursed by the crime of another. Livid, I broke the glass frame hung on the wall of Mr Fidaile's office. I took hold of the sword displayed. I went out to cut off Raymond's head.

I felt something on my shoulder.
"Sir, sir, wake up!"
"Raymond!" I muttered, raising my arm.
I opened my eyes.

A man and a bin bag were facing me. I sat up.

"I 'eard theur shart. You 'ed eur bad dream," said the cleaning agent.

"Where are we?"

"On t' treean. Last stop. Hal'mur."

My destination. I got out of the carriage. An old man was sitting on a bench near the train timetable board.

"Victor?" he asked, getting up. "I am Raymond. Should we have a coffee? I have very little time. We have an appointment at the notary's and I'm leaving at the end of the afternoon."

He looked nothing like the horrible character I dreamed of on the train. It was an old man with a wrinkled face, like any other old man. He no longer lived in Lamheur. Apart from Josiane, all the Putteres had forsaken their childhood village. Work, encounters, and resentment had scattered them. Out of the six aunts and uncles, there remained four. They lived in other areas and would see each other only at funerals. Ten days earlier, Josiane Puttere, a wealthy businesswoman, had succumbed to cancer. She left a fortune to be shared between all family members. The notary was waiting for my signature before releasing the funds. We had an hour before the appointment.

Raymond answered my questions simply. The seven children had had a difficult childhood: a father who fell on the battlefield during World War II; a mother overwhelmed by all these kids. Yvette was a wild child. Starving for attention, she was always under their mother's feet. She hated her brothers and sisters. An unstable teenager, she became pregnant at the age of fifteen, accusing Raymond of rape. He was arrested and spent a few days in jail until his employer proved he was at work at the time of the rape. This incident had been the trigger for family score-settling and old stories were brought back: one had hit the other; the other had locked up the third one; another was accused of theft. A broken family, their mother who drowned during a boat ride, they no longer had anything to say to each other. When I called before my mother's suicide, Raymond had already drawn a line under the incident a long time ago, an incident that had branded this respectable man. Doubts remained about his innocence. I understood the feeling. I had been through the same sort of experience.

"And the baby?"

"Stillborn. It was better that way."

"Who was the father?"

"Yvette had consented. He was a friend... I have said enough now. Sometimes it's best not to stir the memories. Just to see you makes me feel sad."

As soon as the notary's paperwork was signed, Raymond returned to where he came from. When he had refused to give me his address, I had felt a great emptiness. I had realised that I had not made the trip just to revisit the past but also to form bonds.

The hope I was secretly cherishing to cling to my family had vanished within hours. I did not exist and would never exist for them so I had nothing to do in Halemur. Returning to Bonny-sur-Geoy made no sense; I would not find a job and I had no friends there. The train, which should have taken me back home, drew away. The sun set. The last train sped into the night. I curled up on the bench. If I wanted to live, I had to erase my twenty-five years of misery. I erected a wall between the past and the present time. Behind the wall were the memories. None would go through.

When the cool morning woke me up, I had the strange feeling that the night had lasted for an eternity and that the young man who was heading towards the café and then the train station newsagent had nothing to do anymore with the young man who had fallen asleep on the wooden seat the night before.

After a hearty breakfast, I leafed through magazines and newspapers looking for a sign. So many things were written that I was confident there would be at least one which would concern me and help me find a way out. I had no family, no address, and no past. All I had left was a temporary name I would get rid of as soon as a solution would appear, once a destination would attract me. My quest bore fruit. An article recounted the mass exodus of young French people to England, where work was plentiful. After the article, there was an interview with Eric, twenty-five years old, a symbol of success in a foreign land, holder of a business degree, unemployed since the end of his studies but who, after crossing the Channel, had found a job as a waiter before becoming manager of a London restaurant.

At ten o'clock, I emptied my bank account, that is to say 4,321 francs. I was not going to wait for the two million francs of the inheritance because I did not intend to take it. That money stank, it belonged to a so-called Victor and I was convinced that it would bring me misfortune if I was to use it.

From Halemur, I headed towards Calais. In Calais, I made a V-sign at France then I got on board a ship to Dover with the firm intention of changing my destiny. To achieve this, I could not be called Victor anymore, a name I hated, a name synonymous with loneliness, tragedy, failure, a name that was given to me by someone who was neither my father nor my mother, a name that no longer had a reason to be stuck with me.

From now on I would be Erik.

Yes. Erik…

With a *k*.

PART TWO
WORSDEN PANE

1

Freedom

"Erik. My name is Erik. With a *k* at the end. And you?"
"Oscar. Like the Academy Awards."

With small square glasses, a plump face with a mess of curly hair, and wearing a zebra-striped jumper and velvet trousers, Oscar looks like a little boy who just got out of his cage after a long night of rest. He gesticulates in all directions. He speaks. This is his second spell in England. When he was twelve, he had been to Bath with his school and stayed with a family that lived in what felt like a smelly slum. He remembers the stench of the living room carpet and disgusting meals: breakfasts of beans in tomato sauce spread on charred bread with a glass of tasteless milk served at room temperature; barely cooked green beans and small fluorescent peas for dinner. He had found the whole week depressing. The only joy was the day they took the bus early in the morning to go to London, where they stayed for a few hours. People everywhere, street performers, a clown walking in the midst of passers-by and guards in red and black in their funny hats and stony stares standing in front of a large white building.

"Since that day, I haven't stopped thinking about returning to London," he says, overexcited. "London looked completely mad."

"And you're not afraid?"

"What about?"

"Changes."

"I need change. I want a new life. I want to meet foreigners, English girls. I want to become a star."

"Do you speak English?"

"I did English at uni."

"I know the basics but that's all."

"You'll learn quickly. It's not that difficult."

"So you want to become a star?"

"Yeah. I want to become an actor."

While listening, Erik feels his heart beating faster than usual. The boat is pitching. Sandwiches ingested before departure at the port of Calais come back up. A bilingual stewardess hands him a tablet against seasickness, then Erik follows Oscar. They go past the duty-free shops crowded with passengers buying cartons of cigarettes, bottles of alcohol, perfumes and chocolates. Erik lies down on a chair in a huge lounge where passengers eat, talk and rest. He hears a mix of French and English. The British are identifiable by the large number of pints of beer and crisps with different flavours on their tables. They shout, drink and sing, whereas the French quietly sip soft drinks or wine while eating peanuts.

Erik is feeling better. Oscar takes him out on the deck to get some fresh air. The cool wind, the salty smell of the sea, the foam, a tiny speck in the distance: the adventure has begun.

"Where are you from?" asks Erik.

Oscar recounts his last hours on the continent.

*

He is on the platform of Blois station, in the heart of the Loire Valley. He kisses his mother. Lots of advice. She talks incessantly. He boards the TGV, takes his place in the carriage. His mother's lips are still moving. A knock on the window. Oscar comes back down from his cloud, smiles at his mum, and then goes back up, so high he does not understand what the ticket inspector wants. He finally shows him his ticket, would like to tell him he stinks of wine. Calm prevails in the carriage, a few words here and there, the feeling that nothing will happen during the journey. Oscar would like to shout loud and clear that he is about to abandon their world. A world that meets their poor desires, a world that is not made for young people they regard as fools; he is one of these young people and he is leaving this world behind him. Coming from a modest single-parent home, a mum without professional connections – so like the majority of young morons – he had an uphill struggle to find a job. Graduates unable to understand the world of working life, without any experience on top of that... No, being young was not an advantage. It was bad luck. Young people's role was to serve the great masters of money. They had to feel happy to be seen for an interview, to be given hope; very lucky to be called Oscar or Vincent and not Karim or Rachid. Otherwise, the covering letter, no matter how well written it had been, would not be read: a reflex rooted in colonial memory.

Oscar gets up and takes his bag to sit on the floor between two carriages, away from the stifling atmosphere of the compartment. The countryside passes before his eyes. He devours the landscapes he will not see for a while. Tonight he will be in Highgate, North London, in a house located near a big park, a house a childhood friend shares with other young people. He went to the same primary school with that friend he had not seen since then, but as their mothers had stayed in touch, Oscar was able to call his old schoolmate. He was awed by the enthusiasm on the other side of the line. He also found it original to hear him using some *English words* in his sentences. "It's great here, you'll see. Nothing to do with France. Lots to do all the time. When you're in *London*, take the *Northern Line*, the black line. There are *screens* on the *platform*. Take the destination High Barnet or Mill Hill East. When you arrive in Highgate, follow the crowd, get out. You'll see stairs in front of you. Take them. On top, it's Archway Road. Cross the road, *number* 335, bottom bell."

*

Oscar speaks non-stop. Erik listens.

When the captain announces that they are now in British seas and passengers should change the time on their watches, Erik jumps up, claps and hugs Oscar. He does all of this at high speed, in his head. Freedom, finally…

Find Dover station. They set out. It's raining, the wind is frosty, and the two young French men don't understand a word the English are saying.

They are now on the train to London. The next stop is Victoria station. Oscar takes out a pen and a piece of paper.

"Give me your phone number. I'll call you tonight as soon as I'm settled."

"I don't have an address yet," Erik replies.

"Where are you going to sleep?" says Oscar, worried.

"I'll find a hotel. Give me yours instead."

"Are you joking? You're coming with me. I'm sure I can find a way with my flatmates."

"I don't want to be a drag."

"You're not being a drag in any way. You're my guest."

Anxious throughout the whole crossing, Erik now feels relieved. He has a place to stay. He pinches his arm. No, he is not dreaming.

They get off the train, put down their bags at the same time. They are in the middle of people speaking French, Spanish, Italian, English or other languages. Some turn right into the station and vanish. Others turn left. As for the two young newcomers, they remain on the platform for a moment. A corridor, fifteen metres wide, stands before them. They look at the coming and going of a lady in her fifties wearing the words Helping the Homeless over her shoulder. She is holding a box into which many people passing through slip a coin. In France, she would have been mostly ignored. As would have been the tramp slumped in a corner of the corridor outside the entrance of a cheese shop; he is getting some attention as well. A couple turn up. The man and the woman each hold green bags with the name Harrods on them. Oscar knows a little about Harrods. He heard that it was a department store where you could buy a pair of trousers, fishing rods or a banana at ridiculously high prices, the point being to have a memory of Harrods, one of the prides of England.

Oscar and Erik pick up their bags again. They walk through the corridor, coming across an Indian family – three children in jeans, parents wrapped in colourful fabrics – a man running with a briefcase in his arms, a cleaner in blue overalls dragging a bin. Other sweepers are all over the huge station concourse, a concourse with a ceiling made of glass, hard metal and supported by thick iron columns. It is bathed in white light. Some of this light comes from the arch leading to Victoria Underground station.

The two young men have come out of the corridor. On the right, two escalators separated by stairs are crammed with people eager to leave or get to the shopping arcade on the first floor. The second floor is a crowded fast-food area.

After the visit, they come back down. There are train noises and resounding whistles: the concourse is seething with excitement. They try to avoid men and women in business suits carrying black briefcases. Londoners don't seem to notice the fear they cause by walking at an insane pace, opening their mouth only to say "excuse me" or "sorry" without thinking. One of them is sitting at a Burger King table. He seems calm, his nose in a newspaper, the *Evening Standard*. The person sitting next to him, a young man wearing ankle boots and a tight orange jersey, is reading the *Daily Mirror* at lightning speed. He turns the pages as fast as if he was looking at the pictures of a comic book. A woman with crossed legs in a miniskirt browses *The Times*. Most people have a newspaper in their hands. Inquisitive, Oscar buys a few, surprised they only cost thirty pence. Princess Diana and Queen Elizabeth II make headlines in all of them, something to do with a divorce that arouses the curiosity of readers who overwhelm Victoria station kiosks. For those who prefer feeding their body rather than their mind, all they need to do is lift their head. Sellers of nougat, lollipops and chocolate are waiting to sell sweets and confectionery, standing in their stalls in striking vivid green or red. A greengrocer has displayed his products opposite the train departure board, a long board on which two digital clocks are telling the time. It is 6pm.

"Helping the Homeless!" they hear a deep voice shouting. The man, who must be in his seventies, wears the same logo over his shoulder as the lady in the corridor. Dressed in an old brown shirt, a worn green jacket and a dark blue pair of trousers, he contrasts with the youth of a pretty girl standing a few feet away. She tosses the coins she collected for the protection of abandoned dogs into a box. A little farther down, a blind man is asking for money for a blind association. They all want money in this place. A young man has displayed a sign "I'm Hungry".

"Buy *The Big Issue!*" yells a seller of the street magazine, a bearded being with tired eyes and shabby clothes.

Oscar and Erik cross the concourse. They pass a bureau de change ran by four dark-skinned men, sweating in an enclosed space, eyes weary. A beautiful woman with bare shoulders and legs goes down the stairs leading to the Underground and disappears under the lens of one of the many surveillance cameras placed all around the station.

Oscar and Erik follow in her footsteps. They let the colours guide them. The light blue line; change at Warren Street; then the black line. Standing in the carriage, they nearly fall before realising that they must sit or hold on to something if they don't want to be thrown to the ground when the tube brakes.

Highgate. After the escalators, a low ceiling, then the exit, a sort of courtyard, lit by the last sunbeams. Green all around, peace and quiet, steep stairs. At the top, the road, the cars. On the other side, big houses of two or three floors with large windows, shops on the ground floor. The traffic. They look to the left, move forward, the sound of brakes, recoil instinctively, cars pass at high speed. Don't cross here. Find a zebra crossing. The wind rises. Clouds appear. The sky darkens. Drops, and then, almost immediately, rain, torrential rain. At the zebra crossing, they look the wrong way, once again. They are not in France anymore! "Look right," they repeat to themselves. Cars stop, let them cross the road. The rain stops. The clouds disappear, the sky is blue. Their final destination is a bit further up. They walk past a pet groomer, a grocery store selling newspapers, a shop displaying all sorts of things. They go uphill, number 335, ring the bell.

"You're sure I'm not in the way?" asks Erik.

"*Who is it?*" asks a giggling female voice in English with a French accent.

Oscar comes closer to the entry phone.

"It's me, Oscar, Farid's friend," he replies in French.

The door opens automatically. The two young men go inside the building, up the stairs. Second floor. Erik's heart beats fast. Behind the door, he would soon be asked questions. Apprehension is overwhelming.

"Oscar, I'm so happy to see you! *Welcome to London.*"

Farid, whom Oscar doesn't recognise with his beard and probably wouldn't have recognised even if he had been shaved, gives Erik a hug.

"How long has it been? Ten, fifteen years?" he continues while loosening his grip.

"I'm Oscar," says Oscar emphatically. "That's my friend Erik."

All three laugh. The ice is broken.

"Come in. Put your stuff by the *sofa*. That's where you're going to sleep, Oscar. We'll find somewhere for your friend. Let me *introduce* you to Ronan and Elsa. The others will be here later."

The room is huge. There is a double bed, two mattresses on the floor, a television opposite the sofa and things everywhere.

He introduces Elsa to them. She is a petite brunette from Lyon. She puts a small bottle on the coffee table near Oscar's sofa bed, kisses them and bursts out laughing. Before apologising.

"Don't worry, she is seeing someone," jests a young man with prominent cheekbones, a can of cider in his hand. "I'm Ronan, by the way, Ronn to my mates."

He lights up a cigarette and offers them one.

Ronan comes from Rennes. He arrived a month ago with his cousin Estelle, who lived in Evreux.

"She'll be here later. You'll also meet Dam and Oliv, the Parisians. And Modeste, a guy from Toulouse and Natalya, his bird. She's Australian and she's so nice. And Scott the Brit. You'll see. He's awesome."

"We're nine to *share* the flat at the moment," sums up Farid. "We cleaned everything yesterday, but as you can see, we're quite *messy*... Come with me, I'll show you around..."

A long carpeted corridor, Modeste and Natalya's then Estelle's bedroom on the left, the bathroom with a bath tub and the water meter in which you must put a one pound coin for hot water. Then, at the end, the kitchen surrounded by white cupboards, the sink cluttered with dirty dishes, a green plant on the table and, on the side, a door, with stairs leading down to a garden.

"Help yourself to the *fridge*," says Farid. "There must be some sandwiches left from yesterday."

"What do you do in London?" asks Oscar.

"The same as everybody else. I work in catering."

"Are you a waiter?"

"I make sandwiches in the City. It's great. I start early, I finish early and I have all my weekends *off*."

"*Off?* What does that mean?" asks Erik.

"I don't work."

"Did you study catering in France?"

"No. I have a degree in economics. And you?"
"I passed an HND in marketing."
"In Blois, like Oscar?"
"No, in Laval."

Laval is the first town that came to his mind, a recollection of a French lesson on palindromes.

"So you're not from Blois?"
"I'm from Laval."
"They've got a good football team there."
"Yeah. That's my team."

Erik, born in Laval, supporter of the local football team, holder of an HND in marketing…

"All right. So, tonight *you take it easy*. Let's wait till after the weekend and on Monday you can find a job."

"Just like that?" asks Oscar, surprised.

"Yeah. You'll see, it's so *easy*."

"I brought a CV."

"No need. It's all about showing how motivated you are. But we'll talk about it later. Now, *take it easy*. You're at home."

Back in the bed-sitting room, Elsa, a 10 millilitre bottle in her hand, is snorting the liquid, from one nostril then the other; a hush; laughter, hysterical; convulsion; bursts out, howls with laughter; she is out of control; holds her head; calms down.

Footsteps, laughter: it is Modeste and Natalya.

"Modeste had just moved into the *flat* when he bumped into her on the stairs and they've been together since then," explains Farid. "They work in an Italian restaurant."

"How is everybody? Music, maestro!"

Modeste, eyes sparkling from a good time on the stairs, is holding a stereo. He presses the play button. Techno music. Natalya, hair in the wind, light in her flowery dress, is dancing.

"I did the afternoon *shift* and we managed to be *off* tonight. Roll a joint, Ronn. *Party time!*"

Modeste takes off his black trousers and white shirt.

"Do you want a beer?" offers the beautiful mixed-race bare-chested waiter in boxer shorts to Oscar and Erik, who are eating thick sandwiches. They had never tried bacon and chicken together with mayonnaise, lettuce and tomato before, but it tasted surprisingly good.

"Bienvenue dans Angleterre!" they hear shouted.

A young man in a suit, tie loosened, holds out his hand and greets them in perfect French slang.

"Jourbon. Je m'appelle Scott. Et tu?"

Oscar and Erik introduce themselves.

"Je parle français un petit," he says proudly. "Je ai *study* à la *school*."

Alcohol on his breath. As every Friday evening, he had been to the pub with his workmates.

"*Scott! Get your decks. I'll roll a spliff for you,*" yells Modeste in English.

He brings them with records and starts mixing. Loud music.

There's the sound of a buzzer. As all the other male flatmates have done before them, Damien and Olivier shake Oscar's and Erik's hands.

"Chicken masala?" they offer.

The two Parisians from Issy les Moulineaux and Evry, best of friends – "bosom buddies" – work in an Indian restaurant.

When Estelle arrives, the flatmates are all present: Scott is on the decks; Natalya and Modeste are dancing like mad, jumping up and down; Olivier, Damien, Farid and Estelle are in the middle of a long discussion; Elsa is lying on the sofa, eyes closed, head comfortably placed on Oscar's bag; Oscar, tired from the journey and the joints, is struggling to keep his eyes open. Farid shows him Elsa's bed. He lies down fully clothed near Erik, who is watching the show of his life.

"It's crazy here!" he points out to Farid.

"It's like this every weekend."

Buzzer.

"And the neighbours, don't they complain?"

"We don't know them," Farid replies. "Want a smoke?"

Erik takes his first puff of marijuana.

"*Hi, girls!*" screams Natalya while opening the door to two young women in miniskirts. "*We're coming!*"

She takes Modeste's hand.

"Have a great evening!" he tells everybody. "Thanks for the mix, Scott. See you tomorrow."

Decks have been left out and the stereo is on again. The party continues. Oscar seems to sleep peacefully. Elsa hasn't moved. Olivier and Damien are kissing. Scott and Estelle are talking. Farid and Ronan are rolling joints. Erik now struggles to understand what is going on around him. He lies down on one of the mattresses. "I'm in London," he repeats to himself.

Stoned, he falls asleep in the noise and smoke.

A cloud. His cloud, on which he's been sitting since he arrived in England. He doesn't see anybody but feels a reassuring presence, hears soft music, smells a minty scent. He opens his eyes.

"Do you want a tea?"

Erik rubs his eyes. The sun rises. Where is he?

He takes the cup someone has given to him.

"Tu sais moi."

He remembers. It's Scott.

He drinks his tea, eats cookies crumbling in his mouth, smokes what Farid slips through his fingers.

"Wonderful grass…"

Erik looks for Oscar.

"He's sleeping. I tried to wake him up but he didn't stir."

Farid, Ronan, Olivier, Damien, Scott and Estelle are dressed in T-shirts and fluorescent trousers. They have wide-open eyes and are full of energy.

"We went out when you were sleeping. There was a *party* in an old warehouse on Archway Road. A *mad party*. Great techno."

Erik feels tiredness regain the upper hand.

"We'll go to Highgate in the afternoon. It wasn't *expected* but Estelle told me they're looking for a *waiter* in her restaurant."

Elsa hasn't moved an inch. Her head is still on Oscar's bag. Erik rests his on the bed cushion. He feels so happy. Discussions turn to whispers. He falls asleep again.

2

Job

"What really matters is to show that you are motivated."
"But I've never worked in a restaurant!" replies Erik.
Farid reassures him.
"Me neither before *London*. You'll learn on the job."
"And I don't have to show a CV?"
"To show what? That you have no experience?"
"And what should I say?"
"Repeat after me. *I am looking for a job… Are you looking for someone?*"

As the manager of the restaurant where Estelle is a waitress is starting his shift in the middle of the afternoon, Farid, bags under his eyes from dancing all night, takes Erik to Archway, a twenty-minute walk from the flat, an area where he had also brought Oscar late in the morning. Greasy spoon cafés, fish 'n' chip shops and fried chicken fast-food places by the dozen on both sides of the main road, creating an oily smell. A discreet hello to Oscar, busy in one of them. While Farid waits patiently outside, Erik enters. He manages to reproduce the magic formula Farid taught him. As a reply, he is asked to come back later, the next day, and on his third visit, he is offered a job as a kitchen porter. Erik, surprised that in five minutes flat it is possible to find a job, thanks the kind Asian man.

"How much do they pay per hour?"

"Three pounds."

Farid looks at his watch.

"Let's go. Estelle told me to come around three."

Highgate is more pleasant than Archway. Beautiful houses, luxury cars, but also pizzerias, Indian, Thai, Chinese and French restaurants. The one they are looking for is called Le Café Francais. The manager, who is French, invites Erik to sit down.

"You've just arrived, haven't you? What did you do before?"

"I worked at McDonald's…" lies Erik.

The manager thinks, takes the phone from the bar and calls someone. While speaking in English, he writes something on a piece of paper. He gives it to Erik.

"Here, I need someone who speaks English fluently. I wrote down the address of a pizzeria in South Kensington, the French Quarter. Go there tomorrow. The owner is a friend. He needs staff."

The next day, after a second night of partying, Erik goes to the pizzeria in South Kensington, where, as expected, he is offered a job to start in the evening. Farid, who came with him, suggests he keeps looking.

"I have nothing against kitchen porters but I'm sure you can find something better."

It is 11am when they arrive in a small street. Between an Irish pub and Pizza Quick mopeds, there are three tables on the terrace of La Rôtisserie.

"Go inside, show how motivated you are and say what I told you to say. I've got stuff to do now. See you tonight and *good luck*."

Erik takes a deep breath. Since arriving in London, everything he does or says is new. The day before, between two joints, he invented an older brother and parents, owners of a sports shop in the town of Laval.

He enters La Rôtisserie and heads towards the counter behind which a tall North African man dressed in a white chef's coat eyeballs him suspiciously.

"*I am looking for a job. Are you looking for someone?*"

"*Boss, it's for you!*" says the other, wearily.

A stocky, pot-bellied man in his forties comes out of the kitchen.

"*What's happening, Mohammed?*"

"*Him, boss!*" he replies, pointing at Erik, who immediately repeats the magic formula.

"You're French, aren't you? So we can speak French," the boss says in French with an American accent. "Take a seat."

Erik puts Farid's advice into practice and shows that he is lively, motivated and full of energy: he sits down abruptly, almost slipping off his chair, intertwines his hands and looks straight into the man's eyes.

"Have you ever worked in a restaurant?"

"At McDonald's," Erik hastens to answer.

"Where do you live?"

"In Highgate. I arrived two days ago and I came to London to work."

"How long did you work at McDonald's?"

"Six months. But as I moved, I had to quit."

"OK... And are you prepared to come every day?"

The chair squeaks as Erik leans back.

"I'm not scared of long hours!" he states, glancing around the dining room. "At McDonald's, I was doing twelve hours non-stop. I'm prepared to come every day. I want to work."

"Highgate is far..."

"There is the Underground... and I learn quickly. I can start today if you want."

The last point has an immediate effect. The boss gets up and introduces the chef to him. Mohammed has the difficult task of looking after the two rotisseries of South Kensington and Notting

Hill Gate until they find and train someone who can take over the South Kensington job. Erik follows them into the kitchen. Chickens are on the work table, in rows, tied up, seasoned, ready to be put on a spit.

"Can you start right away?"

"Do you mean now?"

"Yeah…"

The boss turns towards Mohammed, speaking to him in English.

"*An apron for the young man.*"

"*OK, boss.*"

"*Train him like you know how to, Mohammed. Train him today and tomorrow. We'll have a chat after that.*"

"*Trust me, boss. He will learn fast.*"

When Erik returns to Highgate on that Sunday, March 30, 1997, he finally has the feeling of being someone. The owner of La Rôtisserie counts on him, and Mohammed, a big Moroccan with tired eyes, exhausted by seventy-five hours of work per week, had kind words for him. He has landed his first job in London. He is twenty-five, but in his head he is two days old. He was born on his arrival in England and he feels that he has his whole life ahead of him.

He looks forward to coming back to his kitchen and his chickens.

3

Girlfriend

South Kensington station. The tube stops. Erik follows the crowd spilling onto the platform. He hears French spoken. It's a group of teenagers. He takes the escalator, standing on the left. Wrong side. He must stay on the right to let people go through. At the top, he takes out his Underground ticket, inserts it horizontally into the ticket-reading machine. The piece of cardboard reappears vertically from the top of the machine. Nothing happens. He waits in front of the barrier. A queue forms behind him. A man with a red peaked cap and a yellow fluorescent vest tells him to pull his ticket out.

It's Monday, nine o'clock. Erik is the only one not to be in a rush. He is early. He remembers his way; he must go straight on. He crosses a square filled with flowers, an island surrounded by a one-way road, with a small green stall looked after by a florist in an apron, scissors in hand. An old lady is raising funds for the homeless. After the traffic lights, it is Old Brompton Road with no end in sight. People are rushing in all directions. Erik turns around. The inscription above the entrance of South Kensington station dates from another time and transports him to a different atmosphere. He walks past shops unknown to him; on the storefront of one of them there are posters of footballers, horses and game scores, and inside, the floor is littered with papers. The sign says William Hill. He passes a health food shop, a music and a luggage shop. An Asian man with a long beard and wearing a turban is putting suitcases on the pavement. Another traffic light. Then the Irish pub on the corner of Old Brompton Road and Bute Street, a street, as he will soon discover, in the heart of Frangland, the London-based French area, with the French Institute, Embassy, Lycée and library. Bookshops, bakeries and some restaurants are also French.

Bute Street.

Erik is eager to start his first job. After passing the tables of the pub, he looks up. A body meets his eyes. It's Mohammed, hands on hips. From his six foot six height, unshaven, dark rings under his eyes, puffing on a fag, he gestures to him to wait. He finishes his cigarette and then beckons him to follow. But getting into the small dining room is not easy. Trying to force his way in with his size, he gets stuck. One last push. He's through. On the left, a long bench sits against a wall decorated with framed paintings of roosters and hens. Mohammed goes right, slipping between the open glass door of the cooking appliance with a rotating spit and the hot counter and refrigerated displays whose racks are still empty.

"Ratatouille on top, gratin dauphinois below. *French beans, green salad* in the *fridge*," he recites, mixing French and *English*. "Hope you understand quickly. Tomorrow I'm *off*. I'm going to sleep. I don't want to be *disturbed*. Hope you're going to stay for a long time. I can't keep on like this. I finished at one last night. I only slept five hours... But it's a great job," he concludes, breathless. "*A great job*."

After the displays, the till. Behind the counter, a high chair, the stereo system against the wall and the phone.

"This is Kylie's seat. She works in the evening."

"Who is she?" Erik asks, intrigued.

"The receptionist."

A last glance at the dining room, supported by white pillars, brown tables made of hardwood with woven straw chairs. At the back, at the end of the bench, there's a mirror in which one can see one's feet, then the toilets and cloakroom, two bags of work clothes and cloths and a guitar on the floor.

Mohammed hands Erik a blue shirt and a white apron, stoops to enter the windowless kitchen. The light is on. On the right is the kitchen porter area, an industrial dishwasher and sinks. On the left, a fryer, a hob and an oven hanging on the wall; a few inches from the floor there are metal cupboards with pots, pans and other traditional utensils. Above, the work table and then the entrance to the cold room, chickens on spits standing straight against the wall, desserts on a shelf, cardboard boxes on the floor. Erik has no cooking skills. Yet, in one day, the master of omelettes, al dente plus five minutes pasta and mashed potatoes whose taste and colour depended on what was in his fridge, would pass from apprentice cook to chef. At eleven o'clock, they eat chicken and gratin, standing in the kitchen. Mohammed continues his monologue. Ratatouille, gratin dauphinois and chocolate mousse recipes.

The tone is more engaging since Mohammed regards Erik as the saviour he's been waiting for for the past two months.

He's told about the preparation of salads, crunchy French beans. Corn on the cob grilled to perfection, club sandwiches not too cooked, the fries, how to use the fryer, changing the oil. Making sure the fridge is always filled with drinks, so there is no shortage of fresh orange juice. The greengrocer located at the end of the street comes twice a week. The butcher situated opposite the rotisserie delivers chickens every Monday afternoon. He's learning to manage a kitchen, as small as it may be, in twelve hours, as the next day he will be on his own to meet the demands of waiters and the regulars, Americans and French families.

Finally, Mohammed warns Erik.

"If the boss's *girlfriend* is around, don't think, just do what she says."

Erik listens to his mentor.

"Don't bug yourself," says a little female voice. "Tonight it won't be busy."

Marie-Françoise is the manager. She is French. She introduces the waiters to Erik: there is Bertrand, or Bert for short, a fellow countryman, Hiro, who is Japanese, and Sandra the Spaniard. At 6pm, two tables are occupied. Mohammed is out smoking. Erik is over the fryer. Tomorrow, he thinks, it will be MY kitchen. He pulls up the basket, shakes it and places the fries on a plate next to a chicken leg. He rushes, is about to pass the doorway of the kitchen, the plate held out in search of a waiter. A head appears. Surprised, Erik steps back, fries and chicken slip from the plate and fall onto the shoes of an unknown young woman. Before he has time to apologise, Mohammed, back from his cigarette break, reappears. He looks suddenly disappointed.

"Don't worry!"

Marie-Françoise wants to be reassuring.

"I'm sure you too broke eggs when you started. It happens."

Mohammed pouts. No, he's never broken eggs.

"Did you have a *break?*" she asks. "No? Poor thing!" she keeps on. "Come on. Out. Get some fresh air."

"If I can't leave him for five minutes…" moans the imposing cook, who then holds the new chef back.

"Take off your apron. There are customers…"

Erik gets out of the kitchen. On the left, someone in a skirt is sitting on the high chair. A young woman wearing a T-shirt depicting a frog is on the phone. She hangs up and introduces herself.

"Je m'appelle Kylie. Je suis une australien. Je suis une *student*."

Then she gives him a knowing little smile.

The shift is finished. Monday, pay day: Marie-Françoise hands out small brown envelopes to everyone, Erik included. Forty-two pounds, his first salary.

"Excuse-moi pour tout à l'heure. Je ne t'avais pas vue."

Kylie doesn't understand.

"*Sorry... for... the accident,*" repeats Erik, but in English this time, pronouncing the *r* the French way and pausing between each word to think about the next one. "*Bang... in ... you. Sorry.*"

She puts a coaxing hand on his shoulder.

"*I love your accent!*" she gasps.

"Kylie, goddess of love! Be careful, my dear Erik," warns Bert, "she's going to hypnotise you... Well, that's it for tonight... I hear there is a party later... Should we have a drink?"

The diners have all left.

"Bert, my sweetheart, can you buy me some tobacco? And take Erik with you. Show him around," suggests Marie-Françoise.

To avoid being hit by a car coming from the right while crossing Old Brompton Road, Erik follows Bert's advice. They return loaded with a few miniature bottles of spirits. They sit on the terrace. Night has fallen; the miniatures have been gulped down; there is the orange light of the Indian restaurant on the other side of the street and a gentle breeze. A haven of peace in a cloud of smoke. They smoke like chimneys. Kylie goes to buy more bottles: three days in London, that's a cause for celebration. Marie-Françoise decides to bring her staff back in. The chairs are stacked in front of the rotisserie. Kylie puts the music on. The room is theirs. Bottles are emptied. Discussions and moods burst out: Bert mocks Marie-Françoise, who takes everything seriously; Kylie indulges herself with Erik's accent; Erik tries to understand Hiro, who explains somehow in basic English livened up with sounds of surprise that before moving to England he lived in a tiny room in Tokyo and made a good living in the building industry. Music in his blood, he came to London to find a band to play with.

"A song, a song!" they shout.

Hiro takes his guitar. Kylie stops the music.

"All You Need is Love" is chosen.

Hiro sings with his guitar. The others join in with the chorus.

Kylie is now sitting close to Erik.

"Be careful," warns Bert. "She's going to jump you! She doesn't get enough sex."

Erik feels a little embarrassed but Kylie's big smile helps him out. Marie-Françoise disappears into the toilet. Sandra changes the music. Techno is put on. Like in Highgate. She pulls Hiro onto the improvised dance floor, whose tables have been pushed against the walls. Bert dances, arms wrapped around the pillar, goes up and down, rubbing himself against the white column. Marie-Françoise dozes on a table. Kylie waves Erik to follow her: they cross the kitchen, go into the cold room. They put their glasses where desserts should have been. She loves desserts. Instead, she savours a French man.

It's one o'clock. Marie-Françoise feels dizzy; Bert is pissed as a newt; Sandra only has eyes for Hiro, who, unfazed, keeps on playing guitar; Kylie straightens her glasses; Erik's fly is open.

There is the noise of a high-powered car engine in Bute Street. The boss comes in.

"*Everything OK?*"

They nod Japanese-like. He counts the money from the till and helps himself from the day's takings. His Ferrari is parked in front of the rotisserie. Inside, a young blonde woman pokes her head through the open window. The engine roars. Gone.

Time to leave. Sandra, Hiro and Bert head for The Fridge, a nightclub in Brixton. Marie-Françoise returns home. As for Erik, he doesn't have second thoughts. Kylie has invited him to her home. They board the night bus, a red double-decker.

"*Two tickets please, driver.*"

They are about to reach the top deck when the bus starts abruptly. Erik grabs the railing just in time to stop himself from falling. As the bus stops, they quickly take a seat at the front. From the first row, the view is breathtaking. The scenery is an array of lights but... they are driving on the left! Shocked, Erik's eyes widen. He remembers with a jolt that he is in England. The bus hurries through Earl's Court, West Brompton, Fulham. Hands clinging to the bar, Erik sees a branch getting closer, bigger, aiming at his eyes. He instinctively heads down, pausing his breath for a moment. Bang! Saved by the roof. And here we go again. Even faster. He looks to the side, feels dizzy. A junction. Prompt braking. The sound of quick steps, a piston, a sliding door slams. The bus shoots off again. They arrive at a bridge. Another screeching halt. Passengers get off, get on. The bus, in its lane, a pavement away from the Thames, revs its engine. A car, in the right lane, has just overtaken it so it starts with a great rush. It's catching up with the car. The gap decreases rapidly. At the end of the bridge, it cuts in front of the car. Horns honking.

"Il est Putney," says Kylie. "Ma village."

Erik, gasping throughout the trip, comes to his senses as he gets off the bus. He kisses Kylie, takes her hand, and lets himself be led through the deserted and tree-lined little streets with sap scents of Colinette Road and Howards Lane.

When they arrive at the door of a huge white house, she asks him not to make any noise. They enter on tiptoe into a large hall, facing the red carpeted stairs leading upwards. On the kitchen table there is a letter from her aunt who lodges her: Kylie's bedroom is occupied by a friend. She has to sleep in the living room. Erik can't stay.

"Come to mine then," he whispers.

She shows him the exit, closing the door softly. They return to Richmond Road, where the bus left them. The window of an old grey Mercedes slides down.

"*Mini-cab?*"

"La taxi," translates Kylie. "Ta adresse?"

Highgate, half an hour away. Words replace gestures. French language. French lessons. French touch. Kylie is attentive. Every word makes her shiver. It's two in the morning but she wants more. The taxi drops them in front of 335 Archway Road. In the bed-sitting room, everyone is asleep: Farid and Ronan on the two mattresses on each side of the bed in which Damien or Olivier is whistling; Oscar on the couch that was separated from the wall to put in another mattress, Erik's bed. The radio plays soft music. The next day, Erik starts working at La Rôtisserie at nine and Kylie has to pop by her house before going to college.

They get undressed, slip naked into the sleeping bag, embrace each other and fall asleep, carefree and happy.

4

Rush

"One *chicken takeaway* with three ratatouille. Two half-chickens, two fries. Three *corns*."

"*One more fries.*"

"Don't forget the chickens in the rotisserie. You must take them out. *Fill* the salads."

"*More orange juice.*"

"*One chicken for table six.*"

"Erik, chickens will burn if you don't take them out now. Come on. We have bookings in half an hour."

"Four *club sandwiches*."

"Replace my fries. They're overdone."

Sweat runs down Erik's face, moistening his lips with a salty taste. Orders keep coming. The restaurant is full. There is no more corn on the cob.

"What do I do?"

"Bert! Go buy some *corn*s. Don't forget the *receipt*. Erik, put the chicken in the *microwave*. Thirty *secs*. *Sandra, you forgot a table. They're not happy*. Erik, when you get the *corn*s, grill them."

Erik passes Kylie's empty chair. The evening was supposed to be quiet. A thick cloth in each hand, he opens the rotisserie's glass

137

door. Heat burns his face. He takes a spit out, puts two chickens on the hot counter and takes the other ones into the kitchen to carve them.

"Start the *dishwasher*. There's no more *plates*. Put a spit in the rotisserie. Or we'll be in the shit."

Erik goes from hot to cold. He comes out of the cold room armed with a metal bar of chickens.

"Stop the rotisserie. If not, you won't manage to insert the spit."

Erik presses a button. The spit stops rotating.

"We have *corns*. Grill them now."

"*Where are my fries?*"

"*French bean salad?*"

Erik checks.

"No more *French bean* salad."

"Prepare some then."

"*Two portions of French beans?*"

"*In ten minutes.*"

"*No! Need some now.*"

"Don't take any more *French beans* orders!" shouts Marie-Françoise. "*No more French beans for twenty minutes.* Bert, did you bring the *drinks* to your table?"

"What else do they want? I've just checked on them. They told me everything was fine!"

"Three cokes and a bottle opener. *The phone!* Can somebody answer, I don't have time. Sandra, *the phone!*"

Marie-Françoise and Sandra look at each other.

"*The phone is ringing…*"

Sandra takes the handset.

"*Do we have French beans?*"

"Erik, how long for the *beans*?"

"They're in the pan."

"*How long?*" asks Sandra.

He didn't hear. A burning smell. The corns!

"Three fries."

"*How long?*" repeats Sandra.

"Don't cook them too much. They've got to be crunchy."

"Two chocolate mousses."

"*Five for me.*"

"Any bread left?"

"*Hiro, can you get some bread?*"

The bottle opener can't be found.

"*Hiro, buy a bottle opener with the bread.*"

"A fruit salad, three chocolate mousses, two *cheesecakes*."

"*One cheesecake and two chocolate mousses.*"

Then it calms down. Erik is drenched in sweat. He swallows a litre of water. Thinks of Kylie, who he didn't see leaving in the morning.

"Well done," praises Marie-Françoise while giving him a pat on the back.

"You're a star, my hero," says Bert.

Hiro looks bemused.

"I am Hiro…"

A phone call.

"*La Rôtisserie. How can I help you?*"

When Marie-Françoise hangs up, she looks nervous. She calls Bert, who follows her out. On their return, she displays a commanding face. Bertrand is standing to attention.

A table for five for 9.45pm.

"A table for five? No big deal. It's not the end of the world," says Erik.

"It's for the *girlfriend* of the boss and her friends."

A deathly hush. Erik has been working for twelve hours. Fatigue begins to be felt. Mohammed's warning is taken up by the walls that pass the buck to each other.

"Stay in your kitchen," advises Marie-Françoise. "Ulrika is on her way. With her, you don't lose your temper. You do what she tells you to, even if it sounds stupid, and everything will be fine…"

The restaurant must be sparkling clean. The tables are covered with red-and-white-striped tablecloths. A candle on each one. A clean sweep. The hens and roosters have a clear view.

It is 10pm. Four tables of two. The table of five is keeping them waiting. The waiters look pale. Laughter is not on the menu anymore. Erik feels his stomach tighten with anxiety. Minutes pass. Half an hour they've been waiting. Maybe she won't come. The phone. False alarm. An order for the next day.

"We have to wait."

At 10.25pm, a blonde, sleek bob, leather miniskirt, followed by four brassy blondes wearing over-the-top make-up and high heels, enters. They step into the rotisserie. The floor vibrates. The pieces of folded cardboard used to fix shaky tables are released from the grip of the legs of the tables which begin to sway under the blows of knives and forks in a sudden hurry. Marie-Françoise replaces them at once. Cheesecakes, fruit salads and chocolate mousses are gobbled by the last diners watching their feet in the mirror. The waiters read their thoughts. Bills are thrown on the tables, banknotes lie in saucers. Falling chairs. Panic. People rush to the exit.

The blonde points towards the middle of the restaurant and asks to speak to the cook. Her friends giggle. Erik is brought in.

"*My name is Ulrika. Ul... Ri... Ka. But you call me Miss Ulrika. Get changed and bring me some gravy. Then go back to the kitchen!*"

Marie-Françoise is standing straight, quite a bit shorter than Ulrika. She translates into French.

Ulrika dismisses her with her hand. "Who does she think she is, this bitch?" Erik asks himself. And to make his point, he doesn't move.

"*Bring me some gravy. Now!*"

Marie-Françoise shows him to the kitchen, imploring him with her eyes to go there. Standing up to the boss's girlfriend is a bad idea. But the chef doesn't intend to let her walk all over him so he sits at the table next to him.

Marie-Françoise is quick to bring him back to the kitchen.

"And the *gravy*, does she want it in her face, this b—?"

"Shut up and stay there."

This is Mohammed who is speaking. Six cooks have waved goodbye before Erik. He knows the score. He doesn't want to play anymore. Informed about Ulrika's plans for the evening, he was on watch in the neighbourhood.

Screeching, with high heels clicking, Ulrika and her friends leave the rotisserie. Calm returns.

5

Party Baptism

Since he started his job roasting chickens, Erik has worked seven days a week, sixty hours a week. But the next day it's his first day off, so tonight he won't sleep. Instead, he will party like his flatmates.

The rotisserie is almost empty. He's going round and round in circles in his kitchen. He can't wait to return to Highgate.

Since coming to London, he's been happy. He has a job, earns a weekly salary of three hundred pounds cash, has a girlfriend who is as sex-driven as he is, and tonight he will party for the first time. His Party Baptism.

He is told he can leave.

In a flash, he is on the tube. A moment later the train stops between two stations. A signal failure, according to the driver. Accustomed to these setbacks, passengers carry on reading their newspapers, chatting or drinking their beer as if nothing had happened. All but three. The delay has sparked complaints from three people: they are French. Their conversation irritates Erik. "Always late in this country… It rains all the time… You can't find anything in supermarkets here... Renting is so hyper-expensive..." They annoy him. He'd love to tell them to shut their face. If they are not happy, they should return to France. If everything is better over there, why are they here? Immature, arrogant expats, morbidly unhappy, they forget that in their beloved country, like most young people, they were struggling. Nobody forced them to come to England. They whine all the time about everything. Whining... a very French trait. Marie-Françoise and Bert are the same. Erik likes them, but when they moan for no reason it sometimes gets on his nerves. They are paid cash every Monday, don't pay any tax and don't make social security contributions and yet they feel sorry for themselves on the grounds that they are not entitled to paid holidays; to compensation when they are ill; to a thirteenth month of pay. Fortunately, that self-deprecation picked up on English soil makes them more friendly. Fortunately, above all, there is Kylie.

When the train sets off again, Erik feels his cock harden. He can't help thinking about his Australian girlfriend. And when he thinks about her, he gets a hard-on. It is uncontrollable.

*

They are at Kylie's. Her aunt is away, in Australia. Out of the shower, they rush, naked, into the garden. He catches her. She is in his arms. He lays her on the grass licking her clit while she sucks him off greedily.

Dressed in a naughty look, open blouse, short skirt, leather boots to the knees, she takes him into a deserted back-alley. The fire exit of a restaurant. They go down the stairs. Erik pins her against the door, lifts her skirt, puts his hands on her bottom, pulls her thong to the side. There's the sound of footsteps above them. Kylie arches her back, he penetrates her, putting on a show for a couple who are watching.

Kylie goes along with all his fantasies. Face to face, from behind, sideways, standing, squatting, kneeling, sitting, lying. They indulge in all sorts of acrobatics. Then they push the game further by inviting a girlfriend. The girlfriend has a boyfriend. There aren't any limits.

So when she tells him they will be separated by thousands of miles, as Kylie is returning to Sydney to visit her family, Erik wonders how he'll survive. Kylie is his drug. She promises they'll make love on the phone and she'll return to London. But then, once she's completed her studies, it may be that she'll never come back.

*

"Please mind the gap between the train and the platform."

Erik rushes out of the Underground. Outside, the weather is mild, the sky is clear, the stars shine. A perfect night for his initiation, his Party Baptism, as his flatmates called it. Despite his questions, they remained mysterious all week about the night's programme. What he knows is that, soon, he'll be part of the gang. Officially.

Erik is in front of his place. As told in the morning, he rings the bell. Oscar answers the entry phone.

"What are you doing here? You were supposed to arrive later. We're not ready... *Wait*, I'm coming down. Let's go to the pub."

And like every time they meet, they give each other a warm hug. It doesn't often happen. Erik is at the rotisserie all day and Oscar works at night. He kept his job at the fish 'n' chip shop on Archway Road for a month but left, disgusted by fish, chips and fried food. He then tried his hand at telemarketing. Far from being a born salesperson, he quickly threw in the towel to become a receptionist.

"In a scouting hostel. I do five nights a week."

"Do they pay well?"

"Eight *pounds* an hour. It's a bit tiring 'cause I don't sleep much, but it gives me time to study. Between *midnight* and six o'clock, it's quiet so I can study. When I feel dead, I lay my head on the table and I sleep a bit... Did I tell you? I've just started a drama and improvisation course in central London. It lasts for five weeks, and if all goes well I'll enrol in a two-year *full-time* course in September. I also registered with different acting agencies, and you know what? The day after tomorrow I'll be an extra in a B-movie. I'm going to play the part of a bodyguard. It's a low-budget production, so I don't get paid, but I don't care. I'm so excited... Can you believe it? My first role."

"How will you manage with your job?"

"As *shooting* is Monday to Sunday from eight in the evening to one in the morning, I managed to get a week *off*. I told my manager I had to return to France for my *grandpa*'s funeral."

"A week is a long time for a funeral. Did they believe you?"

"I told them I also had paperwork to sort out, and as I didn't know exactly how long it would take me and I didn't want to put them in the shit it was better to think big. After all, they're scouts. Scouts know how to get by, don't they?"

"And your studies?"

"They'll email me the lessons. I'll work twice as hard the following week... Anyway, what do you want to drink?"

"A pint of Stella."

"Sorry, but not tonight. You have the choice between a fruit juice and a sparkling soft drink. But no alcohol. We don't *mix*."

"What do you mean?"

"Tonight is your Party Baptism. For your Baptism, you don't drink alcohol. Orange juice then?"

Fruit juice on a Saturday night! Behind the counter, the bartender, who's filling pints with beer, offers them ice and a straw with a condescending look. The bell rings. Last drink. It's 11pm. Oscar pulls out a cell phone from the pocket of his ripped jeans. The green light is given. They go up the stairs to the flat and open the door.

In the entrance turned into a cloakroom, they are greeted by Elsa's most beautiful smile. She gets up nimbly from her chair, goes round a rectangular table covered with an Indian fabric on which, lit by a large cylinder-shaped candle, incense sticks, candy, chewing gum, bracelets, necklaces, balms, and white or black screen-printed T-shirts are spread. She gently puts her lips on Erik's cheek, holds him intensely in her slender and bare arms, pressing her small and firm breasts against his chest, making him feel her hard nipples.

"*Welcome to the world of peace and love!*" she whispers in English in his ear before returning to her seat without taking her eyes off him.

Erik feels drawn by the inviting expression of the petite brunette with wavy hair, almond eyes and a face beaming with goodness. He sees in her a charm that had previously eluded him.

"Who's that for?" he asks.

"We've invited about twenty people," answers Oscar. "We sold them tickets. It will cover the *party*'s cost."

"But for you, tonight, everything is free," whispers Elsa. "Just ask me," she adds, placing her right hand on the picture on her T-shirt, a heart, that begins to beat faster and faster.

Oscar takes his friend by the arm and leads him into the bed-sitting room where the furniture and mattresses have been replaced by a deck, four big speakers and multicoloured spotlights. A huge disco ball hangs from the centre of the room. The walls are covered with rainbow flags and they can hear a Bob Marley song in the background.

"It's wonderful!" exclaims Erik. "But where are the others?"

"In the garden. They're waiting for you. But first, let me show you around, so you'll know where you are if you get lost in the night."

"I can't get lost in my own home!"

"You never know… Farid told me he got lost once."

Dimmed lighting, a mattress instead of the bed, a stereo, sweets on a small table in the two bedrooms, chairs in the first chill-out room, a massage table in the second one.

"*Chill-out room?*"

"A room to relax in," translates Oscar.

"To relax?"

They then go through a corridor lit by fluorescent lights. On the kitchen table and on the floor there are kettles, tea bags, fruit juice cartons and dozens of small bottles of water.

Oscar joins the others in the garden.

"He's coming. He's having a bath," he tells the gang looking forward to induct the one they like to call Mystery Man, since he never lets anything filter out about his life in France. Not only does he not speak about it, but he also doesn't reply when asked questions so that they doubt whether he is from Laval, has a brother and has studied marketing. But they respect his privacy.

When Erik finally appears at the top of the stairs, ten heads rise simultaneously. Hubbub. Cheers. In turn, they give him a hug before sitting down on the grass, forming a U and then a $Ū$ when Erik sits where he is asked to by Farid. The latter takes the floor. The tone is solemn.

"We are *reunited* for Erik's Party Baptism, our Erik, our Mystery Man. We will *share* a moment that will stay forever in our *memory* because it will be unique. In a few minutes, Erik will enter the world of *peace, love and freedom*, our world. Tonight is unique because we will totally open up to Erik. We will *respond* to all of his questions. But before we start, I'd like to be sure we're all on the same wavelength, so if anyone has anything to say, it's the time now."

Ronan raises his hand.

"I've got nothing against the guys we invited but we don't know them. If you want the moment to be unique, why can't we just party between us?"

There's a murmur of approval.

"You told me that a few days ago and I thought about it, Ronn. The *flyers* I was supposed to *distribute* are still in my *bag*. *Tonight*, there will be only us."

"But," reacts Elsa, "what are we gonna do with what we bought?"

"It's for us."

"And all the T-shirts?"

"For us as well. Everything is free... Anything else? No... So, get your spliffs out."

At Farid's signal, the gentleness of the night is lit with incandescent cones. Smoke envelops the eleven young men and women sitting in the garden.

"I *proclaim* the Baptism ceremony *open*," he decrees. "Erik, we're listening to you."

Erik is moved.

"First," he begins, "I'm so happy to be here. I would have never imagined sharing a moment like the one I'm living right now. I would like to thank Oscar for giving me a home when I had nowhere to go and all of you who welcomed me with open arms. As you've noticed, I don't speak about France, and on that topic I would say that before London I didn't exist. Let's say my life started when I took the boat. As I've been working non-stop, I've had no time to really get to know you. I'm lucky to have you, my friends, so now I want to know you better."

There is a question he's dying to ask.

"Why did you decide to leave France?"

The question is simple; answers are a long time coming.

Then there is a silence filled with unsaid things. Since they set foot on English soil, they have not ventured into this grey area. Old pains reappear on most faces.

"I didn't want to send out negative waves..." Erik apologises.

"No harm done," reassures Modeste. "Like you, we all have something to hide. Maybe it's about time to stop kidding ourselves. Me, for example, I had enough. When I was in primary school, I was called dirty nigger, ape, and one day somebody even threw bananas at me. I'm not saying that all French people are racist, but many are. Also, if you pay attention to the use of the word black in

French, you'll realise that it often has a negative connotation. To say you've had a bad year, you are in a foul mood or give someone a dirty look, which adjective do we use? We use the word black. Language is a communication tool that governs relations with others. When a word is linked to so many negative ideas, it is not surprising that the masses have so little respect for someone who is the visual representation of it. How many *black* presenters are there on TV in France? None. In England, there is Trevor McDonald. He presents the ten o'clock news watched by millions of viewers. He comes from Trinidad. Can you imagine a guy from one of the French Caribbean islands like Guadeloupe or Martinique presenting the main French news? I doubt it will ever happen. Or at least not for a long time. Personally, I got tired of France. So fed up I cleared off. And since I've been here, I've never had anybody insult me or disrespect me on the grounds that I'm *black*. At work, they call me *Frenchy*. In France I was called the African, meaning I was lazy, a typical immigrant abusing the system, having a lot of children and smelly on top of that. When I am called *Frenchy,* deep inside I laugh... So Erik, your question definitely didn't send out negative waves. You've asked it at the right time. It did me good to get it off my chest. And I believe I'm not the only one to have suffered injustice in France. You too, Farid, you must have heard so much crap. Haven't you?"

"It's *obvious*. Arabs are thieves, criminals and they don't fit in. Me and my sister, we are third generation immigrants. What does it mean, third generation? We were born in France but we're still not French. We remain foreigners. My grandfather died for France. My parents were born in France and yet my *nationality* has always been questioned. After my studies, I spent two years sending letters to apply for jobs. Nada. No positive reply. Not even an *interview*. A friend *advised* me to stop wasting my time and leave the country. He *explained* to me that his *boss*, when he saw a name or a *surname* that didn't sound European on a CV, it would go straight to the *bin*. In the bin! I am *happy* here..."

"In France, we had jobs but I couldn't stand being called a queen, queer or a faggot anymore. It was hurtful and demeaning," relates Damien, speaking for himself as well as on behalf of Olivier. "I remember this idiot in high school who, as we were having a discussion in a philosophy lesson, had defended the theory that poofs, to use the word everyone uses, had no right to exist since God had created man and woman, not man and man or woman and woman... A good cock in his arse would have done him so much good!"

"Calm down, Dam," says Olivier, putting a comforting hand on the shoulder of his boyfriend. "It's over now. Here we're fine. We even have *Gay Pride*."

Damien had never been able to "confess" to his parents that he liked boys.

"And when are you going to tell them?" asks Erik, who read his thoughts.

"Soon!" he replies, amazed by such perspicacity. "Soon."

"That's what you've been saying for a long time, my love," retorts Olivier.

"You think it's easy? When my dad asks me if I have a girlfriend, I feel in his voice that he knows, but that he doesn't want me to tell him the truth. For you it was easy to talk about it. Your parents are divorced and you never see your dad. If I only had my mum, I would have told her long ago... I'll think about it."

"I also have things to say!" exclaims Elsa. "But first I'd like to smoke another joint. Someone skin one up for me? I still don't know how to roll."

Tongues are loosening.

"In Lyon," resumes Elsa, "there is a large Jewish community and since childhood I've been told I would marry a Jewish man. It works like that between us. If you're Jewish, you get married to a Jew and the only people you see are Jews. When I fell in love with a Catholic guy, I won't tell you how my parents reacted. They brainwashed me, they forbade me to see my boyfriend again, they introduced me to beautiful, ugly, tall, small, clever, stupid, all sorts of boys. But when they tried to convince me to meet this David, whose dream was to become a rabbi, I got scared. I've got nothing against religion but I'm no saint and I didn't see my future as a rabbi's wife. I got so scared that I took my stuff and left Lyon. I haven't been in touch with my family since."

"For me, it was different. Nothing to do with religion. I left because I was no ordinary girl," Estelle blurts out. "When I was a kid, I was more into cars than dolls. A tomboy. That's what I was called at home. I wanted to study mechanical engineering but I was forced to take an economics baccalaureate just because my father thought the world of mechanics was a man's world. I tried to make him understand the passion I had for everything related to cars. He wouldn't listen to me. I failed my baccalaureate twice and then stopped my studies. What was left for me was to get married, have children, look after them and my home and be there for my man. I freaked out. For me, men are not really my cup of tea, if you see what I mean. When Ronan told me he was going to England I followed him."

"You did good, sis," says Ronan. "Your old man helped me a lot when I was in the shit, and I like him, but with you, he messed up."

"And you," Erik asks, "why did you leave?"

Ronan hesitates to say more. Estelle, sitting next to him, gives him a nudge.

"You can trust them."

He lowers his head.

"It's not your fault. You didn't do anything wrong. Come on. Talk. It will do you good!" she urges him.

"I can't…"

"Smoke, it will help you."

Estelle gives him a joint. A few puffs and encouraging words later, he looks up, tears in his eyes.

"Five years ago my parents were returning from a party. My dad was driving and he always drove very fast. He had been drinking a lot. Someone crossed the road. He couldn't avoid the accident. He ran over him and then smashed the car into a tree. My parents died instantly…"

Chills.

"And the guy died in hospital. He was my age," he says, before bursting into tears.

Estelle comforts him.

"After that, I went to live with Estelle," he resumes, wiping his face. "My uncle took care of me like I was his son. But to move on, I needed to leave everything behind…"

"And how do you feel now that you've talked about it?" asks Estelle.

"Relieved," he replies. "It's a bit weird but I feel better."

All eyes then turn towards Oscar, the last French person who is yet to speak. As he has forgotten Erik's question, he turns to Scott for help, looking lost, hoping for a hint that would put him back on track in the discussion.

"And you, Scott, why did you… Uh… Why do you…"

Buying time. So he can come to his senses. This grass goes to his head.

"You see what I mean…"

"Pourquoi je quitter France?" replies Scott in broken French.

"Yeah!" exclaims Oscar, happy to remember Erik's question. "It's your turn and then I'll answer. Why did you leave France?"

They all look at each other. Giggles are coming from his right.

"But je pas français," says Scott.

Laughter spreads. After Modeste, Damien and Olivier burst out laughing. Now all they can hear is laughter. They're all laughing, even Natalya, who doesn't understand a single word of French.

"No more questions?" Farid asks.

Elsa understands. The time has come. From a small plastic bag, she gets out a round, flat tablet on which a swan is drawn. She cuts it in half. Erik has his mouth open. She places it on his tongue. He swallows it with a mouthful of water.

Erik has a knot in his stomach. A mixture of fear and excitement. What is going to happen next?

Oscar reassures him. Everything will be fine. He talks and talks and talks. His sentences become six- and four-foot verses.

But yet we are eleven, says Erik to himself. He looks around and counts eleven pairs of legs, including his own. Twenty-two feet in total. He ponders. He has mixed prose and friends. How silly you are, he thinks. His friends don't speak with their feet... Do they speak with their hands? They use them when they speak. But what they say doesn't become four- or six-fingered hands. Unless... He looks at his hands, counts up: four or six fingers. Six- and four-foot verses it is then.

"The wind undresses me
The rain does make me smile
I am to discover
I have a minder soul."

Oscar, a bottle of water in his hand, bare feet, is playing his part as a bodyguard.

"Under the spot
Under the light
It is a first
I'm an actor."

"*It's a good one... The Swan...*" echoes Scott's voice in the distance.

"*The night is about to start,*" says a voice from the electronic music. Techno trance. Scott, the cowboy of the decks. Hat on his head, lasso over his shoulder, baggy wool trousers and a joint between his fingers, he mixes.

Erik looks at his hands. Trumpet. Cymbals. Drums. The rhythm speeds up gradually then slows down. A teaspoon on metal.

"*Remember we love each other*," whispers the smooth voice. The pace picks up speed. Erik feels his heart beating very fast. Knots in his stomach loosen. A feeling of well-being overwhelms him. Lights of all colours. Lasers. The disco ball rotates. Oscar is next to him. They smile at each other.

"I will always be there for you."

"Me too."

"We will be friends for life."

Flashes. They dance. The room is full of people, last-minute guests.

Jerky lights. Some water. A sip. A small bottle put on the floor. Lost. Found again. Lost once more. Music. Multicoloured dance floor. Oscar is looking for something.

"Where is the bottle?"

"In your hand," replies Erik.

"Strawberry chewing gum?"

"Chewing gum?"

"It's good for your jaw."

"Where is the water?"

"I have strawberry, mango and mint gum."

"This is incredible. The music is brilliant…"

Erik is drinking.

"I want to tell you something," he says, spearmint chewing gum in his mouth.

"Come with me. Let's go to the *chill-out room*."

Natalya and Modeste are locked in a tender embrace. Erik, standing, beats time with his foot. Oscar is sitting on the floor in the corridor, just steps away from the chill-out rooms. He's looking for his cigarettes. Not in his pockets. Looks up. Modeste and Natalya are light years away from where they are physically. He finds his cigarettes in his pocket. The bag of grass. Skins. He finds everything. A lapse. Forgets that skins, grass and fags are back to square one, except that they are in the other pocket. Looks for them.

Birds chirping. The sound of waves. Foam crackles. The sea. The horizon. Oscar and Erik, sitting on a glittering mattress, drink fruit tea brought to them by a fluorescent Elsa.

"Erik, how are you feeling?"

"Great! I want to dance."

"Follow me."

Elsa takes his hand.

Oscar is busy rolling.

"I'll see you later."

A Native American is on the decks. Erik feels full of energy. He lets himself be led to the dance floor. Elsa is opposite him. She is the belly dancer; he is the robot. They're jumping with joy, arms in the air, lifted up by the happy tones of music. Faster and faster they dance, closer and closer they get, perched on the disco ball.

Erik comes down. He changes his T-shirt. Looks for Elsa, who reappears and gives him the other half of the swan.

"I'm gonna massage you."

Erik lies down on the table, Elsa's soft hands on the back of his neck, his shoulders, down his back. Shivers of pleasure run through his body. It feels so good he flies away. Thinks of Kylie. Imagines she's there. She caresses him. They kiss. They hold each other close. She takes him by the hand. They're flying, through the corridor, into the main room. Music, maestro. Modeste on the decks. Sounds and lights. Freeze frame. One second... Freedom on every face... And here we go again! Party! Joy! Happiness! Bliss! Fullness! The seventh heaven! Nirvana! Ecstasy!

Erik and Oscar are sitting next to Damien and Olivier in deep discussion and a couple of strangers who are touching each other gently while dancing to laid-back Arabic music. Leaning against the wall, a bottle of water close at hand, the time has come to tell the truth. A spliff between his lips, Erik inhales a big puff of grass. He trusts his best friend. For the first time since leaving France, he allows himself to remember. His childhood in Bonny-sur-Geoy, the abuse, schools, people he met, the dead. He speaks. Tells almost everything to Oscar. The name of Victor doesn't appear in his account. His name is Erik. With a *k* at the end. As Oscar is called Oscar, like the Academy Awards he's heading for. The sun is rising. Faces look tired. Guests are leaving. Mint tea. Ambient music in every room.

It's eight in the morning. Erik falls asleep with chattering teeth. He hears a voice. Standing on one foot on the spire of the bell tower of a church perched on the Uhuru Peak of Mount Kilimanjaro, he scribbles his thoughts on a piece of paper. The tale of his life is rolled out. One page, one poem. The voice he heard comes from far away. In front of him, there is a door that he opens. Memories escape from it. They fall into the void, into an abyss.

The abyss...

The voice, then other voices echo. Timbres are familiar. Five voices, five people. Twenty thousand feet below, Kimpôl, Freddy, Jung, Oscar and Victor are gathered at the foot of the mountain. They make him a sign to come back down. Erik refuses. He feels so good, up there, on cloud nine.

6

The Return

He feels so good, on cloud nine, that since his Baptism, he is up there every weekend. On Friday, he is in a trance at The Fridge; on Saturday he lets flyers guide his steps; on Sunday, he smokes joints in bars.

"Want some?"

"What?"

Erik doesn't hear. He is daydreaming.

"Want some *smoke*?" repeats Ronan. "I see my dealer in an hour. If you want some, tell me now."

"Get me one ounce."

"What's on tomorrow night at The Fridge?"

"*Return to the Source*. Are you coming?"

"Can't make it. Going to a party in Thyssen Street Studios. But ask Farid. I think he's doing nothing."

Erik calls him. Farid and Elsa enter the bed-sitting room.

"*Return to the Source* tomorrow. Up for it?"

"Dunno," replies Elsa. I'll see how I feel... I'm dead at the moment."

"What about you, Farid?"

"Thanks for the *offer*, but I stopped taking *Es*... *By the way*, be careful. There are some *bad Es* around. They're *mixed* with lots of shit."

Farid is aware of everything. He speaks with ease and knows a lot of people. He doesn't go to techno parties anymore. He isn't the only one. Before him, Oscar had given up. He chose his acting career over partying. "I'm expecting an answer on Sunday or Monday," he told Erik without further details at the beginning of the week.

"Are you working this weekend?" asks Farid.

"I'm working tomorrow all day but then I'm *off*," replies Erik.

When he returns home the next day after his double shift at La Rôtisserie, he is welcomed by silence. There is no one around. He finds a post-it on the kitchen table. Elsa wrote that she would be at The Fridge at around one in the morning.

Underground.

Brixton, and there is no one to be seen in the streets on that second Friday of October. It's too cold outside.

The Fridge, a huge theatre on two floors, is the weekend's starting point for more than a thousand ravers attracted by the psychedelic trance played there. A large semi-circular balcony overlooks the dance floor and the DJ's stage.

The music is at full blast. Hundreds of young people dressed in all colours jump wildly. Erik is going up and up. He doesn't know how long he's been dancing, ears glued to a big speaker, eyes closed, but when he opens them again, Elsa, Damien and Olivier are in front of him. He is elated. He throws himself into their arms. Gives them a long hug with a big smile. The rhythm of the music accelerates gradually. Sounds of far-off tribes. They're back in a trance. They go upstairs, get lost in endless corridors crowded with people; are attracted by lights; go blank in front of a candle. They have a sudden urge to speak and listen. They find themselves in a fluorescent and soothing world with walls covered with drawings and paintings of elephants, Buddhas and labyrinthine shapes. There are pottery, massage, make-up, sunglasses, clothes, sweets and hot drinks stalls. Musicians play djembe, bongo and didgeridoo. Happiness is everywhere. Whether you are twenty or thirty-five, a waiter or a lawyer, whether you like girls or boys, life is beautiful. Then the music stops. It's 6am. The night has flown by too quickly. Ravers head for the exit and flyers are given to them.

And this is only the beginning of the weekend.

"There's an *after* at a friend's," says Olivier.

From Brixton, they go to Vauxhall by tube, mixing with Saturday morning commuters whose half-closed eyes contrast with the three partygoers' wide-open eyes. Damien is wearing sunglasses.

The after takes place in a house. About twenty young people, most of them sitting on the carpet, are chatting peacefully while drinking tea and smoking joints. One of them is standing, leaning over his decks. The music is soft. Erik is speaking with a hippie who gives him the address of a private party in North London. Time flies.

When Erik wakes up, there aren't many people left around. Elsa is lying next to him, eyes open. They return to Highgate where they find Damien and Olivier again. Later on, they'll be back in The Fridge with Estelle for *Love Muscle*, the Saturday gay night. Elsa won't be joining them: she is working.

Erik is on his own, on his way to the address given to him a few hours earlier by a guy he wouldn't recognise if he met him again. At King's Cross, he follows the arrows painted on the pavement. He walks along the fence behind which there is the railway. He has been to this area before.

*

It was in July or August. On a Saturday night. The day before, he had pretended to be sick. Marie-Françoise had given him two days to recover. On Saturday afternoon he was at a music festival in Finsbury Park and had taken ecstasy. In the evening he had taken another one and had danced like mad in an old warehouse in hallucinatory mode, in which drawings on the concrete walls had come out of their frames to mingle with the party.

A great memory…

*

He continues to follow the red arrows along the way.

"Vicky!" he hears calling behind him.

Erik turns around. Nobody…

"Hector!"

He turns around again. Still nobody. Where is he? Music. People passing by. Others speak. He is in a small room lit up with twisted lights of all colours. He has a stomach ache. Feels like vomiting. Looks for the toilets. Engaged. Stands up straight. Turns.

Where is he? He is in this private party in King's Cross… He tries hard to focus. Takes acid. Doesn't remember paying for it. If only there was someone he knew, he would feel better. He takes acid and some more ecstasy. Chews something. Has a joint in his hand. Puffs on it. A bitter taste. He removes his finger from his mouth. He hallucinates.

"*Another one?*"

He swallows another ecstasy tablet.

A hand lands on his shoulder. He jumps.

"*Eight o'clock, mate. Time to go.*"

He didn't notice the time passing. Doesn't remember what happened in the last few hours. He must have fallen asleep. It is eight o'clock but eight in the evening. Outside it's dark. Frozen stiff, he is shivering. He hopes the tube will come very quickly. On Sunday night, there aren't too many. On that Sunday night, Erik, completely wasted, catches the last one.

When he finally arrives at number 335 Archway Road, after feeling sick all the way but managing to hold it, he vomits on the carpet of the entrance.

Then he collapses. Oscar, who has just finished writing a letter for his best friend, rushes out of the kitchen. Erik is huddled up on the floor. He is muttering things impossible to understand. He stinks. Oscar lifts him up, helps him to go to the bathroom, washes him and puts him to bed. As Erik sleeps, Oscar puts the letter on his pillow in which he wrote what he wanted to tell him face to face: the long-awaited answer came earlier today. A positive one. In forty-eight hours, he will meet the team of *Foreigners in NY*, the new US sitcom in which he has been offered one of the five leading roles. His bag is ready. A taxi will be picking him up in an hour. His plane takes off at five in the morning.

Oscar is gone. Kylie didn't return from Australia. Erik feels depressed. After a weekend in which he swallowed almost a dozen ecstasy tablets, acid and magic mushrooms, it took him two days to come down. Marie-Françoise granted him seven days off provided that he promised her to never, ever take ecstasy again, arrive on time at the rotisserie and work in both restaurants the following week to take the weight off an exhausted Mohammed. Erik agreed.

Off for a week. In the daytime, he is alone in the flat. While his flatmates work, he smokes joints and watches TV. Falls asleep. Wakes up in a sweat. Vicky and Hector, two names heard along the railway. The voice seemed so close and yet no one was following him. Did he hear voices? Vicky, Hector…

He feels sad. Kylie landed a job in Sydney. Oscar is in the States. New-found friendships which went up in smoke. Like in France. Freddy, Kimpôl, Jung. And now Oscar. The last time they had a long chat was in June, some four months earlier. It was at his Party Baptism and Erik had unloaded his life story without revealing his real name.

Vicky, Hector…

Had he been caught up by his past, in the space of a discussion?

You can't expect to leave a place and arrive without baggage, can you? Erik, born on a boat, wanted to believe he had none.

Vicky, Hector… Blend the two names together and you have… Victor! The voice heard near the railway was talking to him, Erik, but called him by a name he hated, a name which belonged to the past, a name synonymous with darkness, playing with his mind. So much so that now he can feel Victor's presence in every room at 335 Archway Road. Unable to handle it anymore, he moves out of the flat in Highgate to move into a tiny studio in the heart of Frangland and five minutes' walk from La Rôtisserie.

Erik is back at work. Winter is looming. It is bitterly cold. The road is slippery. The wind is freezing. Ulrika, in a miniskirt, enters the rotisserie and tells Erik to come out of his kitchen.

"*It's time to change the starters.*"

"N'importe quoi…" he replies.

Ulrika doesn't understand French.

"*What?*"

In front of her stands a young former ecstasy addict who doesn't give a damn about her project to change the starters, to replace the Parmesan salad with a Cheddar salad, the green bean salad with a pea salad, the walnut salad with coleslaw. He doesn't care about her salads and states it loud and clear.

"N'importe quoi… *Whatever…*"

"*What?*" she shouts even louder.

Erik loses it. From his kitchen he returns with a Parmesan cheese block, green beans and walnuts. He drowns them in the boiling gravy of the rotisserie. Presses the emergency stop button. The flame goes out. He adds quite a bit of salt and pepper. Rushes to the kitchen. Comes back with a crate full of products: tomatoes, peppers, aubergines, courgettes, ears of corn, potatoes, onions, garlic; frozen fries with the oil in which they should have been cooked; litres of water; ice cream, banana and strawberry cheesecakes. He is about to throw chocolate mousse into the gravy.

"Sacrilege! No, *my friend*, it would be a sacrilege. It's not a Milka chocolate bar with hazelnut, but still, it's chocolate…"

Kimpôl, sitting in the corner of the dining room, signals to him to ignore his presence then disappears.

Erik stirs the mixture with a spit. Takes hold of a ladle. Plunges it into the mixture. Dips a finger in the lukewarm brown yellowish liquid. Having set himself high standards, he pouts. Adds a pinch of salt. Returns to the kitchen. Ulrika, standing in the middle of the restaurant, looks wary. He comes back. A sprig of rosemary. Tastes again. Satisfied, he walks up to her and pours the ladle's contents on her boots. Then takes off his apron.

"*You can lick it, your gravy. And fuck you. Bitch!*"

Outside, he sees a man who launches himself, tearing his hair out. Figure skating. Sliding. Braking. The big tall man falls.

"It's me. Mohammed. Do you recognise me?" The man begs him to listen.

He tried everything to intervene. If it had not rained the day before and if it wasn't minus five, the trip wouldn't have taken so long and he thinks he could have saved the situation. But it's too late. The game is over.

Erik goes home. Back to his stack of dirty dishes, his mess and his bed. He is in his studio, half a mile from Bute Street, a street where there is an Indian restaurant, a pizzeria, a bakery, a beauty salon, an Irish pub, a roast chicken place and a French bookshop. Since it's too cold to go out, he stays at home, sees no one, does nothing else but smoke joints and hide. The appearance of Kimpôl is a sign that Victor has found his track.

After a week in hiding and being as discreet as possible to avoid getting noticed by Victor, money is short. So Erik, wrapped in four layers of woollen sweaters and a large coat that covers the top of his Doc Martens, finds a job in a pizzeria; argues with the pizzaiolo;

quits without notice. He enters a tapas restaurant; takes off his coat; puts on the uniform with difficulty; serves; has a feud with a waiter who pushed him in the middle of a shift and didn't apologise; gets the sack. He's taken on in a wine bar; three sweaters in his locker; serves snails; tells off a disgruntled French diner who left no tips just because "in France we don't tip"; gets his wages in an envelope: in England you don't lash out at customers. Erik changes restaurant as often as his mood.

Spring is coming. He is off for the next two days so he is wandering around South Kensington. Feeling defiant, he steps into Bute Street. The pub's tables, the rotisserie, the blue and red pizzeria mopeds, the smell of grilled meat from the sandwich shop and then of bread from the bakery and, at the end, in the way, the French bookshop's magazine rack. He wants to go around it but accidentally puts his foot between the pavement and the roadway. Twists his ankle. Tries to cling to the rack he drags down with him. Screams in pain. He puts the newspapers and magazines back in their place while wincing. An open magazine lies on the ground. He leans on one foot to pick it up. He is flabbergasted. With a buzz cut, round face and small square glasses, Oscar's face is in *Ici Londres*.

He enters the bookshop, limping, to buy the magazine.

"It's free," says the man behind the counter in French, busy talking with a lady. "It's written on it: '*Ici Londres*, the free magazine for French-speaking expats'."

"Haven't you been taught manners?" yells Erik, angry. "And would it rip your guts out to say hello?"

"I won't have you speak to me in that tone of voice! Get out of my shop."

"I'll leave once you've apologised."

"I'm calling the police."

"Screw you, you and all the motherfuckers of your generation."

He dials 999. One minute later, Erik hears a siren and then three policemen enter. Erik calms down. Apologises for having lost his temper. His name is written in a small notebook. He gets a warning. The bobbies let him go.

Back home, he reads Oscar's interview. His time in London, his acting studies, his experiences as an extra, his luck to have had a teacher who believed in him, the happiness he felt when he learned he had landed the role of the French guy in the sitcom. He then talks about his arrival in New York, a fantastic city ten times more hyped-up than London. Describes the first days of filming of *Foreigners in NY*.

Erik then flicks through *Ici Londres* and reads the classified ads. One of them holds his attention. A company is looking for voice-over artists. No experience is needed.

The next day, he is in Raynes Park, south-west London, in the office of a voice-over agency.

"Practice and come back to us with a sample of your voice, we often need French voices," he is told, "and buy yourself a mobile phone so we can contact you…"

He buys a mobile phone and diction books. When he is not earning his money in a restaurant, he is at home, learning how to speak clearly. "The Crow and the Fox", the fable from La Fontaine. Soon he will burn CDs with his recorded voice and will dispatch them to London-based agencies. He is working hard but he is being slowed down by the distracting presence of Victor, who shows up as he pleases, vanishing as soon as Erik turns towards him. As it happens more and more, Erik has no alternative but to look for a new place to live.

A few days later, Erik calls a cab. He makes sure the intruder doesn't hide in the stitches of his clothes or between the pages of his books. From the heights of Highgate to a short time in Frangland, he continues to go down the map, fleeing the north to go towards the south of London. It's 8.30am, rush hour. The big Hammersmith roundabout is jammed with red buses. The cab is in the fastest lane, but after a brief look in the mirror, he suddenly changes lanes, honking.

There's a long stretch of straight road, local shops, a hospital, green spaces. Fulham, Franglish suburbs, a posh neighbourhood; Putney Bridge; the Thames; Kylie's area. He wishes she was there with him. He has her phone number in Sydney but hasn't dared to call her. He asks the driver to make a detour. The bus stop, Colinette Road and Howards Lane, the house. He's seen enough of it. The cab sets off again. Putney's steep hill, another congested roundabout, the exit towards Wimbledon, imposing properties on the left, a forest and a dirt path used by runners on the right and, a little further on the same side, Wimbledon Common. The car goes right, bypasses the local park. A school, King's College. A residential area. A pub. Cars parked on either side of the streets. Raynes Park. Augustin Road, a dead-end street. Number 26b. His half-house, among other Victorian buildings. The house at 26 Augustin Road is divided into two levels with two front doors, 26a and 26b. The ground floor is inhabited by an old lady and a cat. His new home is located on the first floor. He walks up the steep stairs. A spacious one-bedroom flat. A living room furnished with a round pine table and two chairs. A fireplace. In his bedroom, a double bed and sliding built-in cupboards and a TV. A modern bathroom with a bath and a shower. A fitted kitchen. A washing machine, dishwasher, the same table and two chairs as in the living room. The window overlooks courtyards, gardens split in two. In his half-garden, there are two square metres of grass and two chairs on a deck.

He's taken a big risk. The rent is nine hundred pounds, but on top of paying a month in advance he had to give a two-month deposit, to which was added the application fee and the inventory imposed by the agency. He spent a fortune and all he has left is five hundred pounds cash. But he has a great flat. A flat he wouldn't have been able to get without the help of his former boarding tutor from The Manor of Woe.

*

"Hi Anatole, it's me. It's Er—"

He breaks through the wall. Corrects himself.

"It's Victor," he concedes. "I need three letters of reference and your last three pay slips... And can you lend me some money?"

*

With Anatole as his guarantor, keys in hand, he heads straight for the bank to open an account. The estate agent insisted the rent was paid by direct debit.

After making a photocopy of his ID card, the financial adviser asks him to confirm his name, his place and date of birth. He can't play around and replies:

"Victor Vimord... Bonny-sur-Geoy... 10/09/1971."

Someone repeats his words over his shoulder. Annoyed, he turns around.

"*Are you okay?*" the employee asks, throwing a suspicious look in every corner of the bank.

There is nobody over his shoulder.

"*Everything is fine*," he replies, unsure.

The forms are on the desk, and Erik hesitates. By signing, he will definitely be bringing back to life the boy he didn't want to be anymore.

His mobile phone vibrates. He apologises. Answers. What a surprise! It's Oscar. He will be in London the following week.

Erik signs quickly, deposits his last five hundred pounds in his account, takes a look at the date on the wall. May 4, 1998. He's got work to do. La Fontaine's fables. "The Crow and the Fox". To pronounce as clearly as possible, by opening his mouth well, separating each syllable, breathing in before the start of each sentence, focusing on the text and adding emotion. It is about a crow; a flattered crow; who is too big for his boots since he's so high and mighty; who thinks his shit doesn't stink: it's human, isn't it ? So he starts again from the beginning of the fable. There is a noise. Someone is moving a chair. It's Victor. He is sitting in the living room. Erik acts as if he isn't there but he realises he won't be able to get rid of him like before; at La Rôtisserie and then in other restaurants where he worked, he would be paid and pay his rent and his bills in cash. He didn't have to prove his identity. For his application to be accepted by the estate agency, he had to open a bank account and claim to be Victor.

"Voice-over, what a great project!" exclaims Oscar.

In a leather jacket, shirt hanging over ripped jeans, trainers, square sunglasses, Oscar, the star... For him, things happened very quickly.

As soon as the big party in the Highgate flat was over, he put on a bodyguard suit and, for a week, deep in the English countryside, he protected a London mobster involved in corruption and murder, shielding him against countless assassination attempts, giving it his all, to the point of giving up his own life. Killed by a bullet in the head by the sworn enemy of his boss, who will die too, but from a long death just two minutes before the end credits, the faithful bodyguard, snubbed by the camera, got changed, and then Oscar returned to his studies. Temporarily. Following his first appearance in a B-movie, he had two experiences at a different level, one in a commercial for a war video game, the other in an episode of *EastEnders*.

Very much at ease in front of a camera, Oscar got himself noticed by the headmaster of the drama school who put him in contact with an American friend in charge of a casting agency which was looking for a French person for a new sitcom.

"The first season is scheduled for September. It will hit the jackpot in the US!"

"Should we have a spliff to celebrate?"

"OK... I can't refuse. And you, how are you?"

"All right..."

"I'm still in touch with Farid, and every time I talk to him he asks me about you."

"Is he still in Highgate?"

"He fell in love and he now lives with his *girlfriend* in East London. He gave me a *good feeling*."

"And the others?"

Damien has not only told his family he was gay but he also did it in the presence of Olivier; Estelle made up with her father; Ronan sees a psychologist regularly; Elsa spent the year end celebrations at her parents, to whom she presented Aron, her fiancé, who she met in London; Modeste joined an anti-racism association. They all left 335 Archway Road.

"Now," Oscar goes on, "it's your turn to sort out your life. You can't keep on lying to people and to yourself. Otherwise you won't get anywhere."

Oscar left without knowing any more about his friend, who puts his waiter suit on to provide for his needs, to pay the exorbitant rent of his one-bedroom flat and to pay Anatole back. For the next few months, all Erik does is work. Victor is now always in the flat, but he doesn't speak and Erik doesn't ask him any questions. In July, Erik watches the football World Cup at home. It's a strange feeling. Not only because Victor is sitting next to him but also because he is supporting the national team of a country he can't stand.

In December he quits catering. A voice casting agency he pestered with calls all summer offers him his first job: ten days in a recording studio, six hours a day, paid eighty pounds an hour. Then nothing else. No more calls.

It is now spring 1999 and Erik is skint. He's just paid his rent and has no money left. In a month the bank will debit his account money which he hasn't got. With a joint in his mouth, he thinks about a solution. He doesn't want to hear about catering anymore or make a fool of himself on the phone with casting agencies that have made it clear that the market is saturated with vocal artists. So he is having a chat at home.

"I know what I'm going to do," says Erik.

Outside, it's raining.

"You're gonna find a job," says Victor, speaking for the first time.

"No. I have money in France."

"What money?"

"As if you didn't know… Your inheritance. My inheritance."

"This money will bring you misfortune. You don't need it."

"Oh yes, I do."

"But you don't need bad luck."

"It's only money…"

"That money stinks and I am convinced it will bring me misfortune if I use it. Do you remember?"

"Those are your words. Not mine," states Erik categorically.

"After all…" concedes Victor, "who cares if I didn't earn it by the sweat of my brow. It's our money."

Cannon shot. Transfer. The wall erected on the bench of Halemur station, holed. Francs turn into pounds. Erik totters. His armour, the wall, everything collapses. The two hundred thousand pounds of the late Josiane Puttere in exchange for the return of Victor, the abused child hated by his parents, who turned into a wolf in Kelaindan's grotto, the teenager arrested and handcuffed in front of his school, taken to the police station, the young lost soul, depressed and unemployed. Boundaries between eras disappear, bringing together the past and the present.

Erik is now just a mere memory.

Victor has crossed the Channel.

7

The Bench of Fortune

Stinking rich like Richard Branson, with bags under my eyes and a condescending air, I headed for the Raynes Park estate agency in the rain.

Mike took out a credit card. He spent a sleepless night. An unforgettable party… Celebrated his thirtieth birthday with champagne and coke. Powder on a CD. A twenty-pound note. Rubbed his nose. Looked for his mobile. Five messages. Listened to them. Wondered about the time. It was nine o'clock. Time to go for home deliveries.

At the end of Augustin Road, I turned left. Crossed. I turned right onto Durham Road and found myself face to face with the old lady who lived below my flat. As she greeted me, I looked away, pretending not to see her, and continued my journey. I didn't have to say hello back to her. She was just my neighbour. I didn't choose her, didn't know them, her and her cat. Woken by a strange dream in the middle of the night and then by a pneumatic drill early in the morning, I was tired and in a bad mood. Two hundred yards further to the left, Raynes Park high street. Supermarket, fish 'n' chip shop, kebab shop, newsagent, hairdresser, beauty salon, the agency.

Barman in the evening, delivery man in the daytime, Mike had a clientele of regulars to whom he served cocktails at night and delivered, from ten in the morning, coke, ecstasy, acid, hash and grass. His first customer lived in Wimbledon.

I pushed hard on Yourhome's glass door, which slammed against the wall. The three agents jumped. The woman who had dealt with me previously got up quickly.

"*Mind the door!*" she shouted at me, scornfully.

She put on this haughty air that she reserved, I guessed, for tenants, the little people who didn't have the means to become homeowners, ostentatiously showing jewellery that had probably cost her husband an arm and a leg. I could tell she hated the poor and regarded them as a useless bunch from the way she looked down on me when I was looking for a flat to rent. Maybe she liked my pretty face. Otherwise, she would have told me to clear off and look for accommodation in Shitiflat, a local agency specialising in cheap rentals.

I closed the door very slowly.

After looking at my bank account statement, which was in credit with a six-figure sum, her attitude changed. She had before her a man who intended to buy a house. I was regaled with a sickly sweet "Sir". She poured me coffee in a mug screen-printed with her name, Jane. Her hand brushed against mine. She was at my service. Files on her desk. Phone calls. Emails sent. Having drawn up a list of accommodation likely to fit my needs, she drove me in her four-by-four to a two-bedroom flat located on the other side of Raynes Park station. As we passed the front door of a luxurious apartment, she must have felt my eyes gazing at her round bum that filled her pencil skirt. As she would tell me later, she wasn't used to being looked at this way anymore. Her husband, a TV show producer, had not lusted after her since she had given birth to their second child. Her sex life had stopped long ago and to sense my growing desire drove her out of her mind: she lowered her knickers, put a hand on the rim of the sink and pulled up her skirt. Then she turned her head towards me.

"*Fuck me hard*," she said.

I didn't need to be asked twice.

Mike walked back and forth on the platform, letting his clients know that he would be late. He powdered his gums. The wind rose.

As I left Jane, another storm was looming. In the winter, snow and rain had disrupted the lives of workers and commuters: frozen roads, stranded trains, buses left in the depot, shops and schools closed. Then, heavenly storms had succeeded one another since the beginning of the last spring of the second millennium. Floods had become the most talked about topic in the news.

A heavy shower poured down. Raynes Park station in sight, I ran to take shelter and found myself in the middle of a focused crowd, staring at the departures screen, trains badly delayed or simply cancelled. A businessman who had been waiting for two hours – I was listening to his discussion – offered to start the meeting on the telephone.

"Go back home, you moron," I said to him in French. "You have a day off. What the fuck are you doing? Take off and get pissed in a pub!"

He couldn't hear me. He was working. All the people around me had been working, while I, as Erik, had spent the winter and the beginning of spring glued to the television screen, an ashtray within easy reach, a joint between my lips, watching the world snooker championship, darts and cricket competitions and highlights of football matches from an obscure division, without moving a finger. Just as when I was little and when I would spend hours in front of a wall, arms crossed behind me, on my knees, still.

I fought my way through men and women in business suits, took a corridor leading to platforms crowded with people I shoved to get into a fully packed train carriage due to leave for the English countryside. Three stops later, the driver announced a signalling problem and a wait of indefinite duration.

An hour went by. The news was made official. Due to flooding, most trains were cancelled. There was one which stopped on the opposite platform. There was an announcement muffled by noise. All the passengers got off.

Mike resigned himself to go back home. As he couldn't get to sleep, he ran a bath, got in and dozed off, lulled by the warmth of the water. His phone's ringtone shook him up. His first morning customer, panic-stricken, told him he would make the trip by car. They arranged to meet at one o'clock in front of the supermarket, which was a five-minute walk from Mike's flat.

As soon as I got off the train, I went in search of a restaurant. I passed a covered stall, resplendent with freshness and colours, lettuce, orangey-yellow mangoes, apples, blueberries, strawberries. The greengrocer, a Rasta in shorts, apron around his waist, pointed at them:

"*Try a strawberry, young man, and you tell me what you think.*"
The strawberry was big, juicy and sweet. Delicious…
"*They're cheap. Take three punnets, the fourth is free.*"

With my four punnets in a plastic bag, I walked around a long orderly queue of men and women: Pakistanis proud of themselves, Indians in meditation, Sri Lankans smiling, Koreans with a straight face, English people who looked neither bored nor interested. They were patiently waiting for their turn to enter the post office, under a surprisingly blue sky, an illusion blown by a gust. Blue turned to grey. Umbrellas were opened simultaneously. It started raining heavily. Feeling pangs of hunger, I sped up, walking passed exotic restaurants with spicy dishes, coffee places serving breakfasts, a pizzeria. I dived inside La Famiglia. There were kitchen utensils made of copper hanging in the air. Antiques hung on wooden beams or resting on ledges of fake windows. Old photos in recesses: the national football team, two rows of men in white shorts and blue jerseys, a green, white and red badge above the heart, standing arms crossed or squatting, hands on a teammate's shoulder, grandstands filled with spectators; another photo of the same men, the golden World Cup on the grass, smiles on their faces; a wedding picture; another picture of a large family. The smell of a wood fire. The cosy room breathed happiness.

"Benvenuto amico mio!"

Wearing a chef's hat, a red bow tie and a white chef's jacket showing his potbelly, the short-legged moustached character with thick eyebrows that had just come out of the kitchen, a green paddle in his hand, invited me to sit at one of the tables covered with a red-and-white chequered tablecloth. A waitress brought me a saucer with olives. An accordionist in a white vest top sat in front of the wood stove.

There were mums loaded down with pushchairs in the street. The waitress opened the door barred with a wooden cross. The pizza chef welcomed them with open arms. The musician pressed the buttons of his instrument: a three-step waltz. Children squealing.

A dozen excited kids rushed into the restaurant, without a thought for the customers. The little men started running wild, playing catch, bumping into chairs and tables.

"Le ragazze italiane!" announced the old musician, who looked like the chef's brother.

While adults were eating or waiting peacefully for their pizza, the little ones kept on chasing each other, making their way between the tables. Carried away by their enthusiasm, they eventually knocked over a glass of wine, taking on a guilty look. A frown from the sweaty patriarch, paddle in his hand, ordered the swarm of kids to sit at the table and stay still. If they didn't behave well, they wouldn't have any pudding. Calm returned.

I felt better after a night during which the strange words from a dream had kept me awake for quite some time. I wasn't able to understand the meaning behind them, and I had fallen asleep again but they had not stopped echoing in my head and then they were taken over by the vibrations of a pneumatic drill.

*

"Theeee... doooor... iiiiii... zzzzzzz... oooooo... peeeeeen... Youuuuu... aaaaaaa... rrrrrrrrr... freeeeee... freeeeeee..."

The ground had shaken, my ears had rung. I would have killed the person who had woken me up. I went down to give them a piece of my mind.

"*It is legal, you're doing your job, but it is unacceptable and disrespectful, you oaf!*"

The man had turned off the heavy machine he held in one hand, level with my neck, then had removed his earmuffs. He must have weighed around sixteen stones and I could see rather dodgy tattoos on his left forearm.

"*What?*" he said, in a serious tone.

I had asked him the time.

*

Giuseppe, the owner of La Famiglia, together with his bunch of noisy kids, his grandchildren and those of his brother and accordionist, wished me a good day. It had stopped raining, the air had softened and the sun was making its appearance from behind the clouds. My stomach full, I looked for a bench on the raised kerb of the street that ran through this suburban village, the name of which I didn't know, and in which I didn't know what I was doing exactly.

I didn't go off for a pizza. Led by a dream, I had launched

myself into an indefinite quest of which I wasn't holding the strings, a signalling problem making me land in this place.

What was I expecting from my getaway? What was I expecting from life? What was I expecting from above?

The more I mulled things over, the more I had the intuition that today something would happen, that after today nothing would be the same as before and that it was no coincidence that I was sitting on a bench in an unknown village not knowing what to think.

About the weather, maybe?

It is said that in London, in the space of half a day you can see the four seasons. I had gone through four states of mind in one morning and fifty-two minutes. Awakened by the deafening noise of a pneumatic drill that had pushed me to go outside, frustrated in my pride and faced with a heavyweight, drained by a woman on whom I released myself, unbridled, soothed by the scene of a large family and locals having a simple lunch, I had strung together anger, fear, euphoria and serenity unflinchingly, revealing or confirming at each episode a trait of my personality: I was neither silent nor suicidal; capable of violence, I was sensitive to the happiness of others.

My behaviour was dependent on the environment I found myself in.

Mike had twenty ecstasy tablets in his right pocket, a big block of hash and an ounce of grass for the customer he was waiting for outside the supermarket.

With the road at my back, I sat facing a street, the end of which I couldn't see. I was searching the horizon when, startled by a screech of tyres, I made a sudden movement forward, knocking down my punnets. Strawberries were spread along the pavement. A loud noise. I turned around. Bonnets up, damaged bodywork: two cars had collided.

"Damn it. What a fucking idiot!" Mike thought, his pockets full of drugs. Figuring out that the police would soon be at the scene of the accident, he backtracked, crossed the main road again, walking towards the street where his bedsit was located and at the corner of which there was a bench nicknamed the bench of fortune by the locals because, in the space of two days, a man died there of a heart attack and another became a millionaire by playing a scratch card. Kneeling near the bench, a man, with brown and dishevelled hair, unshaven, prominent cheekbones, was picking up fruit.

Mike couldn't believe his eyes.

"Victor, what the fuck are you doing here?"

This voice... I shouted with joy: "Jung!"

"Do you know where you are this time?" he asked, hugging me.

"Erm... No."

"Were you dropped there?"

"I've just arrived..."

"You're still the same. It reminds me of when you arrived in Laclou..."

Then he looked at me from head to toe.

"You still don't know how to dress, do you...?"

"*Hi, Mike, you all right?*" said a couple who were going up the high street.

"*Hi!*"

"Mike?" I was astonished.

"Just leave it... Anyway, are you gonna tell me what the fuck you're doing in this hole with your *strawberries*? Cause you don't live here. Or I would know. I know everybody in Worsden Pane."

I had no particular reason to be in this place, which now had a name, Worsden Pane, other than the train had left me there.

"And before you took the train?"

I told him about Raynes Park, South Kensington, Highgate; the Channel crossing, Oscar, Erik; my difficult years in France, my mother's suicide, my hasty departure from The Manor of Woe; the address he had given me but that I had swallowed.

"By the way, your brother, did you find him?"

Jung looked at the time on his mobile.

"Have to get back. I'm working in an hour and I've got to prepare my bag. Tomorrow morning I'm off to Amsterdam. I have two days *off*."

"What are you gonna do there?"

"What the hell do you think I'm going to do in Amsterdam? I'm going to pick tulips… You're still away with the fairies, aren't you, Victor."

He adjusted his glasses.

"You're lucky I know you or else I would have slapped your ugly mug… You got something planned for tomorrow?"

I hadn't planned anything for ages.

"Then you're coming with me. The plane takes off at five twenty-seven. In the morning. *Book* a ticket. Meet me at work later and I'll give you my keys. I work at Café Joy. It's further up the *high street*. You can't miss it. *Well*… Not even you."

He checked the time again then left.

As trains were running again, I returned home to fetch my passport, booked a return ticket to Amsterdam at the first travel agency I came to, and then met Jung at Café Joy.

"Too *busy* to talk to you," he shouted, holding out his keys. "Go to 62a No-End Street. Make yourself at home. I'll be done around three."

I fell asleep before his return, dreaming that I met Kimpôl at the Manor of Woe. I slept again in the cab that drove us to the airport. We were in the departure lounge of the terminal.

"Wakey wakey, *my friend!*" he said. "And no *mistake*," he whispered. "As long as we're not in Amsterdam, I'm Mike. As on my passport… Should we have *breakfast?* What do you want to eat? I feel like having something chocolaty—"

"What?" I cut in.

My friend, his two first names and chocolate now… I took a close look at Jung.

"Would your brother's name be Kimpôl by any chance?" I said, hastily.

It was Jung's turn to stare at me.

"No," he replied.

"What's your favourite chocolate?" I insisted.

"What the fuck are you talking about?"

"You did say that you felt like having something chocolaty, didn't you?"

"Yeah! So what? You've never drank a hot chocolate in the morning?"

There was indeed nothing strange in that. I felt ridiculous. I must have been confused and I wouldn't have had second thoughts if, in the corner of his eyes, I didn't see a tear he was quick to wipe away before putting his glasses back on.

He was hiding something from me. In Amsterdam, I would make him talk. I would not leave Holland without knowing the truth. Our paths hadn't only crossed once but twice. It wasn't by chance and I was convinced that Kimpôl had something to do with all this. Or else I was hallucinating and my imagination was regaining the upper hand.

And what if they were brothers, I asked myself on the plane. If they were brothers, it would make sense: the eldest had sent his younger brother on a mission to The Manor of Woe and then to Worsden Pane…

8

Crystal Ball

Jung was offering a spliff to me. We were in a coffee shop. A crystal ball in the middle of the table. Soft music. Apple tea.

I threw a coin in the air. We looked up at the same time. I caught it and put it on the back of my left hand. We checked.

"Tails!" I shouted.

Jung had lost. He took a long puff of weed. He would answer all questions.

"No lies!" I made him promise.

He had accepted the rules of the game. He would tell the truth. Friend's word.

"Kimpôl, he is your brother, isn't he?" I said in a cloud of smoke.

I was so sure he would reply in the affirmative that I was taken aback by his response.

"I don't know."

And he wasn't lying.

"What do you mean?"

"I don't know," Jung repeated.

"How come you don't know?"

"My brother's name was Kim, not Kimpôl. It's similar, but to say they're the same person…"

"Was?"

Unsettled, Jung then pulled himself together.

"I mean, his name is Kim."

Unconsciously, he thought of and spoke about him in the past tense.

*

Ten years had passed since January 1, 1989, when, his most prized possession in his pocket – a train ticket on which was written "Kim, 20 Newman Street, London, W1" – Jung had shown a brand new fake passport to a maritime customs officer. The ferry. England. London. The town centre. Soho. Then 20 Newman Street. Bitter disappointment. Instead of accommodation, there was a recording studio. He had rung the bell. Recognised by his accent, they had sent him a French man in his thirties with long hair, a large checked shirt, torn jeans and old trainers.

"Sorry, mate. Don't know any Kim."

"This place, has it always been a studio?"

"For the past three years."

"And before?"

"Before, it was a flat."

"Who was renting it?"

"Come in. I'll get the boss."

Fifteen minutes later, Jung had the name, the phone number and the address of the former owner, someone called Paul. He lived within walking distance. On the way, he stopped at a phone box. Mister Paul's number was no longer in service. As for his address, it was a squat. Since he didn't know where he would spend the night, he set up home, staying there for a week. He then moved from squat to squat, meeting a lot of different people to whom he would ask, in the event they came across

Kim, to send him to Charles Peguy Centre in Leicester Square. It was a centre for French speakers looking for a job or accommodation, where Mike, since it was the name he was using from then on, had set up his headquarters. The staff had become accustomed to his daily presence.

His last memory of Kim dated back to when he was about eight years old. He couldn't give any description of him so there was little hope that someone would send his brother to him. Over the following months, then years, he spaced his visits to the centre, until he decided not to go there anymore. Neither at the centre nor in any of the many squats he lived in would anyone ever receive a visit from his brother. But he didn't lose hope completely. Their reunion had to happen but somewhere else and in other circumstances. He forsook his bohemian life. After five years occupying buildings without any legal rights and not giving a damn about the future, he found a job as a bartender at Oxygen, a trendy bar located close to 20 Newman Street, and moved into a thirty-square-foot bedsit above the bar.

There had to be a reason for this address to have been written on this train ticket. He would scour the entire neighbourhood in search of clues.

But work and parties took over his time. Working as a bartender from 6pm to 3am, he supplemented his income by dealing all kinds of drugs in the daytime. People would call Mike at all hours.

One evening in July 1998, exhausted by three years of working, going out and getting wasted, he decided to put Soho behind him. He no longer had the strength to stay there. He wouldn't see his brother again, and what represented his most prized possession, he would burn it.

He walked to his bedroom window. People were singing in the streets.

"And one... and two... and three zero... World Champions, World Champions, we are, we are, we are champions..."

He closed the window and didn't mingle with the celebrations that took place in Trafalgar Square. That night, while French flags were waving at Nelson's feet, Jung prepared for bereavement. He was holding the train ticket and a lighter. He read the address slowly and for the last time – 20 Newman Street – looked sadly at the small piece of cardboard that had made him come to England and given him the hope that one day he would hug his brother. It was of no use anymore. He turned it around, brought the flame closer and was going to burn away his nine years in London when his eye was attracted by something he hadn't seen before. Hypnotised by the address on the back, he had not thought to look at the front. There, the name of the station where the ticket was bought was printed. It said Worsden Pane.

Not wanting to repeat the same mistakes as in the past, he didn't rush. He had a job and a home this time so he put his plan to leave Soho off until later. What he needed was money. When he had enough money, he would use a private detective.

The following winter, he moved to Worsden Pane.

*

"His name is Kim," Jung repeated.
"Who gave you the address?" I asked.
"I don't know."

He had found the train ticket in his jacket pocket at the time he was sleeping rough. It was a few months after he had run away from The Manor of Woe and before he had visited me.

I took a sip of tea. Jung passed me a joint.
"By the way, did they catch you?" I asked.

*

Manor of Woe, November 20, 1988

Chased by the police backed by the army, Jung had hidden in the nearby huge forest, eaten plants and mushrooms, hallucinating and sleeping in the bushes, biding his time. There was no way he would go to jail. Yet there was no getting away from it if he was arrested. Several counts were hanging over him. The bakery robbed of all its sweets would make one smile. Robberies of a clothes shop, a grocery and a petrol station would be a great reminder that there had been despicable precedents and that he was on police files. The indictment would tell of a long list of offences. Between the time when he lit a cigarette and the time he tossed away its butt he had created disorder and confusion in the village of Laclou, helping himself to the tills, filling his bag with clothes and preventing addicts of American crime television series and westerns from reacting by putting his gun to their head. Click! A squeeze and they would die too young. At least that's what they thought, frightened by this foreign thug dressed in black, with a scar on his ominously composed face. For the record, the terrifying metal gun he was holding, he had stolen it a cigarette earlier, fifty yards away from where he was, gleaming under the lights of a toy department in a small supermarket. Jung was a delinquent and challenged the established order, but he wasn't a cowboy.

*

"I handled things so they didn't nick me. In the forest, I found *mushrooms*. They were good, but nothing like the Mexicans I have here."

In the palm of his hand there were small, orangey and shrivelled mushrooms. He told me to mix them with my tea and then swallow slowly, while chewing well.

"It's kind of weird that we have both changed names," said Jung.

"The three of us with Kimpôl," I added.

"A chocolate cake?" he offered.

I rubbed my eyes. Through the crystal ball, I had just seen strawberries on the bench of fortune. I passed my hand behind it. There was nothing.

"Should we go?"

I followed Jung into the street.

We approached a bridge which swayed as we set foot on it. It was the right weather for a stroll, a river or a land ride – it was sunny – so it was crowded and noisy. We passed on the other side of the bank, sat down on a log, facing the Amstel. Big and small boats and gondolas were sailing past. We watched a dugout canoe steered by men in business suits and launches loaded with guys wearing a beret. Then we saw beautiful women in red riding past on tall bicycles. I looked to my right. Jung was no longer beside me. He was standing on a raft. I jumped on it. Then we sat down next to each other and we let ourselves be led, carefree. We knew we would eventually return to Worsden Pane.

As soon as we came back from Amsterdam, Jung went to work, leaving me alone in his flat. I fell asleep, peacefully, with the TV on.

There was a murmur of voices, quietness and then the sound of a chair falling, my heart beating faster. I pushed a door. I yelled.

I woke up in a cold sweat, petrified by what I had just seen in my sleep.

I saw Jung in the silence of his bedroom, facing a television turned off, arms dangling, a smile on his lips, eyes closed, a rope around his neck, hanged…

9

Oddfellows Close

Jung was devoting his time to nothing but work. He would start his shift at 5pm, return home between two and three in the morning, get up at eight, go out on delivery and be back at Café Joy at 5pm. Seven days a week. He had to work hard as his Soho savings went up in smoke, and in the autumn he was planning to travel to South Korea to track down a distant cousin who had fled the North.

We didn't get to see much of each other, so when the opportunity arose I got straight to the point. My premonitions of the death of Augustin le Fonbou and then of my father had come true. I didn't want to lose my friend.

"You've never wanted to kill yourself, have you?"

Jung stopped counting his fifty-pound notes.

"Kill myself? You're out of your mind, *man*."

"What will you do if you don't find your brother?"

"I haven't started looking for him so no point in going further."

"Promise me…"

He cut the discussion short. He had other plans in mind.

"Should we eat in the centre? In Trafalgar Square, I know a Chinese place. You pay ten *pounds* and you eat what you want. And then, as we never see each other, we'll go to a bar and a *nightclub*."

I sensed his anxiety all evening. At Eat As Much As You Want, at World Café and at Dance Floor, several times I caught him looking lost after staring at a diner, a drinker or a dancer who reminded him of his origins. He was in a bubble: he let in dreams which would disappear into thin air at once. I could have left and he wouldn't have noticed. I also stared at tall guys who could have been Kimpôl.

"Tell me about Kimpôl," he asked me in the mini-cab that was taking us back to Worsden Pane.

I told him about his appearance in the Pyrenees.

"When was that?"

I couldn't forget the summer my father had died.

"July '85."

His jaw dropped.

"Do you remember what I told you at The Manor about Father Broniel?"

Armed with an iron bar, he was about to smash someone who had messed with him, when Father Broniel had stepped in, preventing him from committing what would have been the biggest mistake of his life.

"I always thought my *brother* had something to do with this intervention. That also happened in July '85. Did you see him again?"

"At the start of the following school year."

"When I got my arse in The Manor! And then?"

That was on my last day at La Rôtisserie.

"Uh… Last year…"

Or was it the year before?

"When exactly?"

"In the winter."

"Yes…?"

"It must have been in December."

It was definitely in December but…

"Early December, mid-December, late December?" he enthused.

I got it wrong. It was the previous winter, but he was so animated that I didn't dare spoil his excitement.

"It was mid-December."

"When I arrived in Worsden Pane! And after?"

"That was the last time."

"Do you know how to draw?"

Jung paid the driver, who dropped us off in front of 62a No-End Street.

"Draw him for me."

I snorted another line of coke and I drew a tall character which took up the whole sheet: a shaved head, eyes, a nose, a mouth and ears.

"You studied art, didn't you?"

"No, I did a technological baccalaureate."

"And they didn't teach you how to draw?"

"I was rubbish."

"I can tell."

To this poor imitation of a drawing, I added that when Kimpôl had appeared in the rotisserie in South Kensington, we didn't have a conversation; at Bonpomme's secondary school, he had told me he was studying in London; in the mountains, we had spoken only about me.

Jung wouldn't get anything else out of me. He went to bed. He had to get up at eight.

It would be our only evening together in six months. He had his project. To carry through with it, he didn't allow himself any fun, working very hard and saving money as if his life depended on it. Meanwhile, I was having a whale of a time.

Every day, I would meet up with Jane.

She told me that she had taken this job as an estate agent to fill what had become a boring life, since, from won-over woman, knocked up a second time, she had become a burden. With her loaded husband, a TV producer, she had rubbed shoulders with celebrities, smiled and shaken hands with hundreds of individuals, whether they were talented or not, drunk champagne freely, flirted, exchanged phone numbers she would call on the sly the next day, shown off her jewellery to play who's the hottest tonight, bitched about the behaviour of the one nobody knew the name of, railing against the young wannabe who was trying to overshadow her. Jane wouldn't have missed those receptions for the world. Then the birth of the first one; six months' break; an au pair hired. Festivities resumed. The clichéd driver, with a hat, white moustache and grey hair, brought her back intoxicated and on her own many a time to the dwelling that was her castle. Then there was the birth of the second child.

"Children need their mum."

That was according to the producer who had it off with the young wannabe. Jane, the stay-at-home lady of the manor, glamour put aside, was invited no longer, the party over, forgotten. She became an estate agent. It was her turn to have some fun.

We attended the Cricket World Cup in London, the Wimbledon tennis tournament finals and the Formula One British Grand Prix at Silverstone in the best seats. I didn't know a bloody thing about cricket, but as I drank champagne, I didn't feel guilty. Jane also took me to spas; we spent a weekend in a five-star hotel in the green county of Kent and another one at the Hilton. I was living the life of one of those guys who, in the movies, just have to snap their fingers to get what they want, a lord in the making.

We also visited houses in Worsden Pane. For one hundred and fifty thousand pounds, I hoped to find one to my liking. Parallel to No-End Street, wider and tree-lined, Oddfellows Close attracted me straight away with its very English buildings and large windows, difficult to close, with worn-out joints, allowing the cold from outside to penetrate. The house in which I was about to enter had just been put up for sale. Smaller than the others, it was at the end of the cul-de-sac and had no direct neighbours.

"*Where's the kitchen?*"

We had gone through the ground floor without coming across a single object. It was a single room with neither walls nor kitchen.

"*First... floor...*" Jane said in a naughty tone.

She was irresistible at times like this. But banging on the door stalled my enthusiasm.

"*What's wrong?*"

"*Did you hear it?*"

"*No.*"

"*Someone's at the door.*"

"*I didn't hear anything.*"

"*Just stay there. I'll be right back.*"

I crossed the empty carpeted space and opened the door: nobody. Oddfellows Close was deserted.

Jane pulled up her knickers.

"*First floor*," she said in one go, disappointed.

The upstairs also surprised me. A bath, a sink and a toilet were the only furniture. As on the ground floor, there were no walls, and the big room, whose floor was covered in an old purple-blue carpet, was bright. Daylight poured in through six curtainless windows, three on each side of the room. I was puzzled.

"Is there a garden?"

I dreamed of a large wild garden. We went downstairs. The back door opened onto a vast green space full of nature, high grass, flowers and brambles: a long-abandoned garden. Love at first sight. I had my dream in front of me. Attached to the house, the garage served as a kitchen.

"*Quite unusual... But who lives here at the moment?*"

All Jane knew was that the house had been rented for years and now the owner was in a hurry to sell it.

10

Broken Into Pieces

"Worsden Pane, soon in the hands of a mysterious zillionaire?"

This title was on the front page of the *Worsden Guardian* dated September 10, 1999. The free local newspaper arrived in my letterbox just a few seconds after I had entered my new home.

Intrigued, I started reading the article. It talked about a wealthy Russian, American, Qatari or Chinese stranger who had chosen Worsden Pane to build a modern city. I didn't think much about it. The press loved that kind of idle gossip. Then someone knocked on the door. I wondered who was visiting me. Apart from Jane, nobody knew that I now lived at 15 Oddfellows Close. It was her, indeed, in a state like never before. She rushed in.

"*I couldn't wait.*"

She removed her fur coat and put a hand on her belly. Three positive tests had confirmed her pregnancy and I was the father of the baby. I welcomed the news with a smile. I was going to become a dad, something that had never crossed my mind. I was still only a son, even though I was the son of two dead people.

"*I'm married,*" Jane said in a hysterical voice. "*I can't keep it.*"

"Why not! Leave your husband. Come and live with me."

She had no doubt about the sincerity of my words, but she knew we would regret it and have issues from the moment the first difficulties arose. For her, abortion was the best solution.

"*You do that*," I warned her, "*and I don't want to see you again.*"

I asked her to think it over. She replied that she had already made arrangements.

Two days later, she was lying on an operating table. My child was broken into pieces, his little head squeezed, his whole body sucked into a tube. It instilled in me a resentment towards this woman who was no better than my mother.

"The shock of my life," I explained to Jung.

Two weeks had passed since Jane's visit. I had not stopped thinking about my son or my daughter who should have been born in six months. I wasn't against abortion as a matter of principle, but since I was directly affected, I considered it murder. Jung set me straight.

"What do you think? That you bring up a kid like that? Wake up, nutcase, and stop talking bullshit. You don't need a kid. Look after yourself first and then you'll see…"

I changed topic.

"And your project?"

"I'm off to Korea on the fifteenth of October."

Jung was no longer working at Café Joy. Before flying to Seoul and meeting up with his cousin, he was planning to use the three remaining weeks to delve into the local town hall, library and the *Worsden Guardian* archives, looking for any clues linking his brother to Worsden Pane.

"Do you follow the *news* at all?" he asked.

"I don't have a TV and I don't buy *newspapers*."

"Have you been out of your house since you moved in?"

"I went to the supermarket."

"Did you not notice anything between your house and the supermarket?"

"No."

"Do you need glasses or what? Did you really not notice anything?"

"Nothing particular… What is it?"

"So you don't know what's happening at the moment?"

"What's happening at the moment?"

"Get dressed and come with me. You'll see."

He took me into streets parallel to Oddfellows Close, at the end of which he would ask me, for each of them, if I had caught sight of anything unusual. All I could see were houses.

As we walked up the main street, he would point at flats above restaurants and shops. When we got to the church, the highest point of the village, he looked at me.

"So?"

With no reaction on my part, he took me to the other side of the high street. Children were having fun in the school playground. Further down, passers-by were coming in and out of shops and then there were many customers in the three estate agencies. We stayed for quite some time in front of each of them.

"So?"

I didn't see what he was getting at.

"Look carefully at the addresses of the properties."

I took a closer look. Wimbledon Park, Raynes Park, Berrylands, Hampton Park, Park Royal…

"There are many parks around…"

He pretended to slap me.

"At least you're not blind… So you didn't notice that there are no houses up for sale in Worsden Pane?"

"It can happen…"

I ducked to avoid getting slapped in the face.

"Was it the same when you were looking for a house, you idiot?"

For sale signs outside houses and flats were all over the streets. I remembered it very well.

"And do you know who bought them?"

To avoid saying something stupid, I kept quiet.

"A guy, the same guy, loaded with *dosh*."

"Loaded with what?"

"*Dosh*. It's Cockney."

"Cock what…"

"Cockney, dickhead. Slang. What planet do you live on? Cockney is a London slang. Everybody knows it… Anyway… It's a guy loaded with *dosh* who is buying them all."

So the local newspaper's headline wasn't a hoax. There truly was a chance that Worsden Pane would soon fall into the hands of a multimillionaire who wanted to build THE city of the third millennium.

"Why here?" bounced back the *Worsden Guardian*. In response, employees of the local newspaper were given the choice to cooperate or change jobs. It was written in black and white on a memorandum signed by their new boss.

No one knew why this stranger had chosen this Woodbeeshire village. Most Worsdenpanians didn't give a toss. They had received a visit from a door-to-door salesman who made them an offer twice the value of their property or business, which they accepted happily, rubbing their hands. As for tenants, they were offered six months' rent paid on the day of their departure.

"You'll still be there when I return, won't you?"

Jung's childlike tone moved me.

"Of course I will. I'm not leaving my close."

"And you don't do anything stupid, right? Once is enough. Now, you leave married birds alone and you find yourself a woman."

I promised. His phone rang. He answered and then left it on the table. The mini-cab was waiting in front of 62a No-End Street.

"I'm going to miss you," he said, before clutching me to him, hugging me strongly.

"I'm really going to miss you, *my friend*. You're quite fucked up but I love you to bits."

The cab driver opened the back door of his old Mercedes. Jung got in. My heart began to beat faster. I had a bad feeling.

"You should sta—"

The car had started. The window was open. Jung was waving goodbye.

11

Guilty

Jung's departure coincided with the beginning of a national debate. Stemming from a one-of-a-kind situation, and a first in the UK, it was the takeover of an entire English village in the midst of barely contained applause from its inhabitants, who were signing for the death of their community – the debate didn't last long.

The number of residents and independent businesses, which had been decreasing since September, fell sharply. In three months, from eight thousand, they became eight hundred, and La Famiglia remained the only independent trading name.

There was still a vote in Parliament, but it was a formality. On December 4, 1999 at 9am, in front of 10 Downing Street, the prime minister announced the news predicted by national media. The "Yes" vote had won. That decision taking effect immediately, Worsden Pane was officially no longer part of Woodbeeshire county, the London suburb, England or the United Kingdom. It became autonomous. The prime minister reminded journalists present in Worsden Pane that, as their safety was no longer guaranteed by Her Majesty's police force, they were strongly advised to leave.

On-site, cameramen who were filming the last images of the village followed this advice. They turned off their cameras and put them in trucks. At 10am, there were no more reporters to be seen in Worsden Pane.

At 1pm, calm and cold reigned over the village.

Wrapped up in a duffle coat, I hurried on. I was hungry. I entered La Famiglia.

"Benvenuto, Vittorio! *How are you?*"

Giuseppe greeted me in the same usual jovial tone. He didn't seem to have been affected by the day or the previous weeks' events. The good mood he had always shown on each of my visits was sincere. I guessed he had been that way since he had opened his pizzeria in the sixties.

He proudly showed me a photo of the youngest of his family.

"*Born in Paris last week...* Che bello! Molto molto molto bello!"

He kissed the picture of his grandson.

"Una pizza quattro formaggi, *as usual*," he said, asking me to sit at my table in the middle of the restaurant.

I used to hate cheese, but since I'd moved to England, I couldn't live without it. I loved Cheddar, especially melted on jacket potatoes, over pasta, in a toasted sandwich with ham and in Giuseppe's four cheese pizza, my favourite pizza.

I sat down. The restaurant was full. The customers were my age but I didn't recognise anybody. At the table next to mine, a corpulent young man devouring a pizza with pepperoni looked up and stared at me with interest.

"French?" he asked, his mouth full.

"Yes," I replied.

"Me too. Been here for a long time?"

"In Worsden Pane? Three months."

"Me, I've been here for one month. I have a permanent contract."

"What do you do?"

"I'm a negotiator at the moment."

"Who do you work for?"

"I dunno but they pay well. And meals are included."

"Do you often come to La Famiglia?"

"For lunch and dinner. It's in my contract."

"Where are you from in France?"

"A village in the countryside. You probably don't know. It's called Bonpomme."

"What?" I exclaimed.

"Bonpomme."

"Of course I know. I'm from Bonny-sur-Geoy."

"That's incredible."

But true. What a small world.

"I have family in Bonny-sur-Geoy," he said. "My cousins run the butcher shop."

"The Largraus?"

"Yes."

"How's their father?"

"He's dead. He was a heavy drinker."

He took a huge bite of pizza.

"I came to England for that job. I was on the dole in France and I couldn't find anything. So when the employment agency in Bonpomme offered me this very well paid job, I took it. I was gobsmacked because I have no experience in negotiation. I speak a bit of English but I'm not great. And there were lots of candidates. I didn't even have an interview. I was selected on application and they paid me six months upfront."

"Is it still... What was his name? You know, the guy who worked in the agency."

"Simon?"

"Yes. Simon. Does he still work there?"

"No, he left. He moved to the South of France with his wife and his son. To Marseille, I think."

"So you know Geneviève?"

"A bit. We were in the same school when her dad was the headmaster. I'm a year older than her. Did you also go to the same school?"

"Not long, but I did."

He stopped eating, staring at me.

"Victor? Is that you? Victor Vimord. How could I forget? I remember about you now. Everybody knew you at school! I knew you reminded me of someone. You were the star of the school. We didn't dare talk to you... I can't believe it..."

"What happened to Mr Pinson?"

"He didn't stay. I heard he won the lottery and he went to Africa to help orphans. It was a rumour, I can't say for sure."

"And Mrs Vermur?"

"The one in charge of discipline? She became headmistress but now she's retired."

"Between her and Mr Riotte, you know, the history teacher, there was no love lost."

"That's why she found a way to get rid of him. As far as I know, he was transferred to a tough school near Paris. Poor guy..."

"It must have taught him a lesson. What a bastard, that teacher!"

"He's dead. I heard he killed himself."

"Sorry?"

"He's dead. My dad told me he was found hanged at his home a few months after his transfer."

Despite disliking the history teacher, I felt saddened by the news.

After Guillaume Tell's staff, I asked about the three pupils I had a vivid memory of.

"Hogan works as a bouncer at Hulk, Bonpomme's nightclub, where you have fights all the time."

"Jean-Sébastien?"

"The one you hit? I was in the corridor when it happened. Good God, he took so many beatings! And not only from you. He annoyed everybody. I think he was given such a hard time at school he moved to another town..."

"And Elodie Chanelle?"

"Did you know her well?" he asked, on the defensive.

From the tone of his voice, I guessed that he, like all the boys at school, had been in love with Elodie.

I had not forgotten the cool lips of the first girl I kissed, the fruity scent of her skin, the naughtiness in her eyes, the words she whispered to me as too intimate to be heard by others. If there was someone from that time I wished I could see again, it would be Elodie.

"You're not going to believe it but she also got a contract to come here. And yet she wasn't unemployed. She had a beauty salon in Bonpomme."

"Do you have her number?" I hastened to ask him.

He put his hand in his pocket and pulled out a mobile that was vibrating.

"It's my employer calling me. I've got to go now."

"Her number!"

"Can't be late or I'll lose my job."

He stuffed the rest of the pizza in his mouth, got up hurriedly and went off in a rush. His departure was followed by the departure of all the customers, who disappeared one after the other after also putting their hand in their pocket and answering their phone. Giuseppe told me it had been like that for the past three months.

"Amaretto?"

He put the glass of liquor on the table and sat down with me.

"By the way, Giuseppe, the guy I was talking to, do you know his name?"

He didn't know. He also didn't know who was the billionaire who had sent the same salesman twice, offering him a large sum of money, and even more on his second visit, if he agreed to sell his pizzeria. Each time, the discussion had been courteous and the representative had stated that he was under no obligation to accept the offer.

It had been the right move, since his turnover was up. His suppliers had changed: he now only had one since the greengrocer had sold his business, just the one from whom he ordered everything he needed and at a cheaper price. His only regret was to have lost customers he had seen growing up over the years. But he got used to these changes and had no reason to complain.

"Questa è la vita."

That was life, and life in Worsden Pane was going on through good and bad times with its new people and a new face that I discovered while walking on the high street under a sky covered with a thick white cloud. Not far from La Famiglia, there was a place with no name that served English breakfasts, and on the other side of the main road, except for the supermarket, everything else was shut. Then there was the town hall. Fixed on its façade, two digital meters showed the numbers 292 and 85. A man who was passing by told me they corresponded to the number of inhabitants and people employed by the village's owner, in real time. When 85 became 67, he added that the contract of eighteen of his colleagues had run out and they had therefore left Worsden Pane. From then on, every time I passed the town hall, I would look up to follow the demographic and labour force changes in the village, paying particular attention to the remaining number of employees, hoping Elodie Chanelle was still one of them.

After my walk, I went to the supermarket. It offered a new service: same day home delivery. As I hated shopping, I decided to fill my fridge and my cupboards with as many groceries as they could possibly take. I filled three trolleys with non-perishable food and frozen products. In the electrical department, I ordered a big freezer and a laptop with an internet connection. I was going to spend so much money that I was asked not to queue. Sitting on a chair next to a security guard while a cashier was scanning and an assistant was bagging my shopping, I watched people pushing their trollies on the screen. Was I hallucinating or were some of them familiar to me? A couple, the man, tall, thin and bald, and the woman, small, plump and redheaded; a one-armed teenager with a messed-up face in a wheelchair trying desperately to grab a football; a man in his fifties nervously leafing through a big book about war; a woman choosing knives, hand on her belly. Before disappearing from the screen, they pointed at me through the CCTV camera. Then a cameo appearance. In the chocolate department. Kimpôl! He winked at me and then disappeared.

Shaken by so many bad memories, deeply distressed to have seen Kimpôl, as if he was one of their own, at the same place as the people who had reminded me of my parents, Augustin le Fonbou, Patrick Riotte and Jane, I paid for my shopping, trembling. Gripped by fear, I returned home with great strides, in the night and under the snow which was beginning to fall, and I locked myself in. I stayed hidden upstairs under my bed without moving until I heard the sound of an engine. Checking carefully through the window, I saw a van parked in front of my house. There was a knock on the door. I went downstairs.

"Who's that?" I shouted, to show I wasn't scared.

"Your delivery, sir."

"Can you tell me what I ordered?"

"You've ordered a lot of stuff, sir."

"When did I place my order?"

"Today, sir."

"At what time?"

"What are you playing at, sir? It's your delivery from the supermar—"

"Please tell me at what time I placed my order."

"Well… It was four hours ago, at 5pm…"

"OK…"

I was going to open the door when I had a doubt. What if it was a trick? Some ghost coming back to take revenge on me…

"Sir," the voice said, "I have a few more jobs to do tonight. I can leave your delivery by your door. It's just that if you want me to connect your freezer…"

I took my courage in both hands and opened the door. The man was no ghost. He made no comments on my behaviour, as if he understood how afraid I was. I took him to my garage-kitchen, in which he dropped off bags full of food. He fitted the freezer next to the fridge and the cupboards I had recently bought. He then followed me into the house. Upstairs, he connected the laptop to the internet and then left.

Alone once again, I lay down on my bed, made a few joints, dipping into Jung's supply of hashish and grass he had given me before leaving for Korea, snorted a long line of coke and swallowed two Valiums. Dawn was breaking when I fell asleep.

When I opened my eyes, it was dark. The only light came from the laptop. I didn't remember switching it on and even less to have put it on a page displaying the weather forecast. It announced that between four and eight inches of snow had fallen, though it wasn't snowing anymore anywhere in the country. I looked out of the window. It was way off the mark. My garden was covered with a twenty-inch white layer and a snowstorm was raging. I made myself a cup of tea, which I drank sitting on the carpet and typed *weather forecast Worsden Pane* on the keyboard of my new computer. The search didn't match any documents. I checked the spelling. All the words were spelled correctly. I searched again but without quotes. No results found. I replaced *Worsden Pane* with *Woodbeeshire*. A list of towns and villages appeared on the screen. I scrolled down. No sign of Worsden Pane. That was weird... One thing leading to another, I discovered that it didn't appear on Woodbeeshire county maps or any page. I lived in a place that didn't exist on the web? This didn't make any sense. Besieged by doubt, an idea came to my mind. Jane could prove the existence of Worsden Pane since she had visited me. Her decision to have an abortion had left a sour taste in my mouth but she was my closest link in time with the outside world and I was willing to get over it as I needed to believe that the information read on the web was wrong. I got my phone.

"You've dialled an incorrect number. Please check the number and try again."

She must have changed her phone number, I thought. I called old friends. Same result. Wrong numbers. All of them. Jung's mobile. Straight through to his voicemail. Worried, I called individuals and companies found on the net. The same tune again and again. Maybe my mobile wasn't working properly. I changed my means of communication. I was sure I would receive at least one reply to my emails. I sent one to my contacts.

Delivery error. This user doesn't have an account.

Had all my contacts changed email address? I was puzzled. I then browsed popular websites, clicking on *contact us... Delivery error...* The same message was automatically returned to me. It was just baffling. I went back into my inbox. Zero unread email messages. I clicked on the spam folder, which would usually receive about twenty unwanted emails daily. The last one was dated December the fourth. It had been sent at 8.59am, one minute before the prime minister announced the loss of Worsden Pane.

I gave it my last shot, even if it meant incurring the wrath of my interlocutor: I dialled 999, the emergency number, accessible to all phone owners. But not to me.

I felt guilty. It was surely not a coincidence if, overnight, a village in which I had just settled in had been completely isolated and wiped off the map. It wasn't about a political decision. There was a culprit and the culprit could only be me. I was the cause of the abandonment of Worsden Pane as I had been the cause of my parents' death, a student's killing, a teacher's suicide and my child's murder, as the ghosts of the supermarket had reminded me. They had all pointed at me as the guilty one.

What had I done or had I not done for Worsden Pane to deserve this extreme punishment?

The more I thought about it, the more I was convinced that I should have never bought this house. I should have followed my instincts and left that cursed inheritance. Such was my fault. There was no one else to blame but Victor Vimord.

Child of ill omen I had been. The man I had become was also sowing misery all around him.

12

No-End Street

For fear of causing another human tragedy, I shut myself away at home, knocking myself out with drugs while the outside world was getting ready to celebrate the beginning of the third millennium with mass rallies and extraordinary fireworks.

Suddenly I heard someone ordering me to get up. It was the same voice that had driven me out of my house in Raynes Park and put me on the way to Worsden Pane. I felt myself go.

I was in my garden. It was buried under powder snow which came up to my neck. First I entertained myself by throwing snowballs against the window panes. Then I made a misshapen snowman with which I began a discussion. He didn't reply to me. Of course, I said to myself, he has no mouth. I drew one with my finger.

"Snowman, listen to me."

What an idiot I am! He couldn't hear... I drew him ears.

"Snowman, can you hear me?"

He moved his lips.

"I can hear you but I can't smell the cold."

I put a nose on his face. He sniffed.

"You stink! Don't you ever wash yourself? Who are you?"

I drew him eyes which started to blink.

"What a beard you have!" he exclaimed. "If you think you're Father Christmas, it's a bit late. He's already been."

"I'm not Father Christmas."

He looked closely at my face.

"Of course you're not Father Christmas!"

He stared wide-eyed as if he had missed something.

"Father Christmas doesn't give poisoned gifts – not him! You, you are Victor Vimord... Make me become powder again, please..."

"Do we know each other?"

He closed his eyes.

"Who doesn't know the one responsible for all the ills in the world? Please, make me become powder again. Don't make me become an accomplice to your actions."

"I won't harm you. I just want to talk."

"Talk to yourself. Make me become powder again."

"I can't."

"Is there anything you're able to do at this moment in time?"

"I can talk to you."

"Do you really have something to say?"

"I have lots of stories to tell."

"I'm sure they're horrible. I don't want to hear them."

He paused.

"I don't want to be cursed. Every year I bring happiness to children and they will also be cursed if I listen to you."

I protested.

"I have no intention to harm you or your children."

"This is not what I can see, man of ill omen..."

"Is that really what you think of me? That I bring misfortune?"

"That is what I can read on your face. Have you looked at yourself?"

I looked at myself in the mirror. *Victor Vimord* and *Cursed* were ink-written on my forehead and my chin. I took some snow and erased the writing, which reappeared but on dotted lines this time. This snowman with no arms and no legs would become powder again only when I decided.

"As you're Heaven-sent, you will help me to understand what Heaven wants from me."

"You're wrong. Your salvation won't come from Heaven."

"Where will it come from?"

"Let's make a deal," he suggested. "I'll give you a piece of advice and in return you make me become powder again. But promise me that you will keep your word."

"What advice?"

"Give me your word first."

I promised. I swore and then I made him an arm and a hand that I shook.

"Get out of your garden immediately."

A ringtone sounded out in the house. The snowman had done his part so I kicked him hard, making him into powder again, and then followed his advice. My phone was upstairs. I rushed in but it was too late. I had a missed call from Jung. I called him back and got his voicemail. In five minutes, I could be at his home. I opened the front door. The view was blocked. On tiptoe and with my arms horizontal and perpendicular to my body, I stepped forward. Then, mimicking propellers in motion, I made my way through the dusty snow. As I reached the end of Oddfellows Close, I had to stop to catch my breath. Blackout. What was I doing in the middle of the snow? What day was it?

"You're lacking stamina, marathon man!" said the big cloud over my head.

I blushed with shame. A runner of my level winded by a helical hundred metres! I had trained so hard in my teens, sometimes until I puked my guts out. And I got titles. French running champion. World Champion. Olympic Champion. If I had kept on competing, I would have won the Intergalactic Championship.

"But you left sport behind," pointed out the grey cloud. "What a pity!"

"I didn't leave anything behind," I replied, annoyed with such an underachievement. "And I'm going to prove it."

I returned home. I put on shorts, trainers and a vest top and began to run in the close. Slowly at first to warm up, I then accelerated gradually. After about a hundred round trips, I stretched out. Back in, I had a bath. I was hungry, very hungry. I washed and shaved. I prepared a night feast: three huge jacket potatoes, six cans of baked beans in tomato sauce and a kilo of grated Cheddar cheese. I stuffed myself. My belly full, I found it difficult to get out of my garage-kitchen. I felt so heavy that I lost my balance. My nose in the snow, I crawled towards an igloo when...

I opened my eyes. Lying on the bed, I was covered in sweat. The laptop was on. Live broadcast.

"Three, two, one... Happy New Year! Happy 2000! Happy new millennium!"

There was a jubilant crowd on the screen. Hugging and kissing. Fireworks. Explosions of happiness.

I got up, went over to one of the windows overlooking the garden. Below, there were footsteps. As I looked down, I saw the reflection of my face: I was shaved. On the floor I noticed an object.

"Jung!"

I picked up my mobile. The battery was flat. I put it on charge. Went downstairs. Opened the front door. The snow had been trampled from one end of the close to the other. I entered my garage-kitchen. There were jacket potato leftovers on three plates, open cans of baked beans and an empty bag of Cheddar on the table. I crossed the room, went out into the garden. There, I recreated the scene as I recalled it. I threw snowballs against the window, made a snowman with eyes, ears, a nose, a mouth, an arm and a hand. I questioned my creature. It didn't answer me. I was waiting when I heard my phone ringing. Time to go back in and upstairs; it was too late. One missed call. It was Jung. He was back in Worsden Pane. Five minutes later, I was in front of his home.

The keys were in the lock of number 62a No-End Street. I entered.

There was a travel bag on the floor in the entrance. I stepped over it.

There was a letter addressed to me on the living room table. I put it in my pocket.

There was a silence in the corridor. I pushed the bedroom door.

Jung was sitting on his bed, his phone between his legs, the sleeve of his shirt rolled up, a needle stuck in his swollen arm and his face was pale. His eyes opened briefly. When they closed again, I could hear his voice.

All my life I dreamed of seeing my brother. I went to Korea to find him. My cousins told me that I had never had a brother. My life has no meaning anymore. It has never had any anyway. I fought for nothing. I no longer have the strength to keep on.

I'm sorry, my friend.

I let go of the letter I was holding in my hand and walked up to Jung. His heart was no longer beating. He was dead. Jung, my friend, was dead.

Then I heard his voice again, but distant.

"You're still there, you motherfucker? I told you to clear off!"

I left him, silent. I felt guilty. I had promised him I would be there for him when he came back but I didn't answer his call. I was responsible for his death as I had been responsible for many deaths. A baby. A teenager. Adults of all ages: men, women, close or not. People who loved me or could have loved me. People who hated me. In France, in England. Misfortune followed me. I could have lived in the depths of the jungle; men would still have died because of me. Guilty all down the line. I had to stamp out this curse. Wipe myself off the face of the world. Kill myself for the good of the living.

While millions of people were making New Year's resolutions, I walked alone in the snow with one thing on my mind: to die. "Your salvation won't come from Heaven," the snowman had told me. "Where will it come from?" I had asked him.

As I passed the bench of fortune, a noise on the other side of the high street made me turn. Half a dozen people were running towards me, bottles in hand. I looked down.

"Happy New Year," they said at the same time. "Whisky?"

I took the bottle, which was full, and I emptied it with my head thrown back, witnessing the sunrise.

"Gin?"

In front of me, five completely drunk strangers collapsed in the snow. A woman with a familiar face stood in front of me. My heart began to beat intensely. Jung's death, alcohol and the appearance of this woman overcame me. I burst into tears. Then I fainted.

13

"I'm here. I'll take care of you and everything will be fine," whispered a soft voice.

Was I in Heaven?

"You slept for three days non-stop," said the female voice.

I struggled to open my eyes. I could see a young woman stroking my face. My body quivered.

"It's me, Victor. Elodie. Do you remember me?"

"Elodie?"

"You fainted in my arms."

"How…"

"Leave questions for later. We'll speak when you've fully recovered. Now, I want you to take it easy and let me look after you… You must be hungry."

I passed my hand under my pillow, where my drug box was. It wasn't there. I panicked.

"Given the state in which I found you on the first of January, I flushed it all down the toilet. That stuff is extremely bad for your health. Now that you have me, you won't smoke any more dope, and you won't take cocaine or Valium ever again."

"But…"

"There is no but. Where's the kitchen?"

When she returned, a hearty breakfast on a tray, I was so incensed by what she had done that I tried to send it flying. I only managed to make it fall out of bed. She didn't get offended. She cleaned the floor. Too weak to get up, I screamed, draining myself of what little energy I had left.

"Give me a line. Where's my coke? I want coke. I want a joint. I want meds. Where are my meds?"

Exhausted, I fell asleep. When I woke up, Elodie was sitting on the bed. She told me to wait. Moments later, she was feeding me. A spoonful for Victor. A spoonful for Elodie. A spoonful for…

She stayed at my bedside for the next few days, until I was drug-free. Every morning, she would ask me to clear my mind and think only about positive things, like the return of spring. As I put weight back on again and looked fitter, she started taking me for a walk in the garden where the snow had melted.

It was after one of these walks that we made love for the first time. Then I told Elodie everything about my life. She listened closely to me all day.

"What a story! It was so lucky that we met that night, otherwise who knows, maybe you'd be dead. Just thinking about it gives me the creeps."

"By the way, what made you decide to come to Worsden Pane? You had it all in Bonpomme."

"I had everything and nothing at the same time. I had my beauty salon, which went well, my friends, my routine and a quiet life."

"So why?"

"Because I love you. I fell in love with you at school. When you left, I felt very empty inside."

"And you've never met anybody else you loved?"

"I've had boyfriends, but it never felt the same as with you. You must know that you were my first love, and I quickly understood it, the one and only. In your arms, I felt special."

"What was special about me?"

Elodie smiled.

"I must admit that, at school, I was attracted by your bad boy image. Over the years, it was the memory of our kiss in the playground."

I was flabbergasted. Someone had loved and thought of me all these years.

"So you came to Worsden Pane because you cared for me?" I asked, warily.

"Yes. And I haven't regretted leaving Bonpomme behind," she added.

"OK, but there's one thing I don't get. How did you know you were going to find me?"

"I was told I would."

"Who told you?"

"Mister Paul."

"Mister Paul?"

"The big boss. The owner of Worsden Pane."

"Can you describe him to me?"

And to my surprise, she described Kimpôl.

"Did he tell you anything about a brother?"

Elodie stopped me.

"It's all in the past. The future is you and me… So, shall we have a pizza?"

Her arm around mine, we walked with a light tread to La Famiglia.

There was one digital meter left on the town hall's façade: it showed the number zero.

"There are no more negotiators," said Elodie.

"It means you lost your job then!"

"It doesn't matter. I have you. And we both have savings. Who needs a job? Shall we go?"

The last pizza at La Famiglia. Giuseppe told us that he was returning to Italy. Business wasn't good anymore, he was tired and he missed his family. His children had followed the great departure last December and all he thought about was joining them, taking a well-deserved retirement and enjoying his grandchildren. He gave us his address in Como – "near Milano" – and told us he would be expecting us to pay him a visit in the near future. We wished him all the happiness in the world and went back home, too much in love to be sad.

I still couldn't believe it. Since my school years, I'd had someone, who was now a woman, who had never stopped thinking about me. Life was beautiful. Happy in our cocoon, we had each other and that's all we needed. The only outdoor place we would go to was our garden, where the grass was growing. Food was delivered to us. We didn't care about what was going on in Worsden Pane. We would have a candlelit diner, sleep, wake up and spend our day together. Gradually, my wounds healed. If bad thoughts came to my mind, we would sort them out by talking. The future belonged to us and it was out of the question that a third party, a memory or a fear would disturb our peace and quiet.

When, on the first day of spring, Elodie told me she was pregnant, I was beside myself with joy. I stopped smoking, started sport again and looked after the mother-to-be of my child.

"Don't you find it weird that it's always cloudy? In four months, I haven't seen the sun, not even once," said Elodie, whose bump was growing.

"Are you happy here?" I asked.

"I'm happy to be with you but I want to live somewhere else. Our baby will come soon, and I want him to have a normal life."

"So we'll leave."

"You'd do that for me?"

"For the three of us."

"Do you feel ready to face the world?"

"With you, I am ready for anything. We'll sell the house and we'll leave. And even if we can't sell it, we'll still leave."

"We will sell it," Elodie claimed.

"How can you be sure?"

Elodie looked grave.

"I'd promised you we would never talk again about that Mister Paul."

"Don't worry. I'm fine now, and it's not just about me anymore. It's about the three of us. What is it about him?"

She seemed relieved.

"Before leaving my beauty salon, he gave me his business card with his email address on it and he told me something I didn't really understand at the time but which makes sense now. He told me to contact him when the time comes, ask him whatever I wanted and he would accept it."

"So?"

Elodie reread with a contented look the reply she received almost immediately after sending the email.

"Mister Paul is buying our house. And he's buying it for twice its value. He's asked me to meet him today at two in front of the town hall."

It was 1.30pm.

"It's in half an hour! I'm gonna get dressed quickly and—"

Elodie cut in.

"He asked me to go there on my own. It won't take long."

We hadn't let each other out of our sight since the first day of the new millennium, so I suddenly felt extremely anxious about letting her go.

"Everything will be fine, Victor. And soon we'll no longer be living in Worsden Pane."

Her eyes lit up.

"What about leaving tonight?" she said, exalted. "Where should we go? I don't want to return to Bonpomme. Actually, I don't want to return to France. What about living in Italy? Giuseppe could help us settle in."

I was listening to her, petrified of being separated from her. If anything happened, I wouldn't be able to save her. Somehow I hid my anxiety.

"We'll go wherever you want, as long as we're together and you're happy."

"Could you bring me some crisps?"

For a month, she'd had cravings for salt and vinegar crisps. I had eaten the last packet before lunch.

"I'll order some now."

I called the supermarket. As we were regular customers, the manager agreed to have a big pack of crisps delivered to our home.

"Look! Mister Paul has sent another email, but this one is for you… I have to finish getting ready now…"

I clicked on the message addressed to me. A document was attached. Download time: three minutes.

Elodie was ready. We went downstairs. I held her in my arms at length and then let her go, a knot in my stomach, looking at her walking away.

"Elodie!" I shouted.

I caught her, hugging and kissing her as if it was the last time.

"Don't worry. Everything will be all right. And tonight we'll be somewhere else. You, me and our baby. I love you, Victor."

As I replied "I love you", the words rang true.

When Elodie disappeared at the corner of Oddfellows Close and the high street, I began to regret not having accompanied her. My phone rang. It was her.

"Victor, I have to hurry. My battery is almost flat. Prepare the bags, and when I return, we'll take a taxi and we'll go to London. We'll spend a night in a hotel and then we'll have plenty of time to decide on our next destination. I miss you. I lo—"

The communication was cut off. I climbed the stairs. The file had been downloaded. I opened it.

Victor,

My mission is about to come to an end. I booked a cab. It will pick you up later on today. When you're inside with your sweetheart, I will vanish into thin air and you will stand on your own two feet. You'll never hear from me again because you will no longer need a guide. That's what I've been for you all these years. A guide.

What a long, complicated and treacherous journey it has been. However, you've shown tenacity, and the reward is now within your reach. You have an incredible woman who's always loved you, and your child will have the best mum and dad in the world. There is much talk today of genes being passed from generation to generation. Let me reassure you. Yours are different from those of your parents. Your son or daughter will be proud to have you and I know they will be able to rely on both of you whenever they go through difficult times.

Your need to understand in order to move forward – and God knows, raising a child is demanding – requires some explanation. You remember when I appeared in the mountains, at the school in Bonpomme, at La Rôtisserie in South Kensington and more recently at the supermarket in Worsden Pane?

I would show myself every time you were in a critical situation. The death of a father you wished you had killed with your own hands, the woman of your life you didn't dare kiss, chocolate – my guilty pleasure – that you were about to mistreat, and, more seriously, the madness of thinking that you were guilty of everything that happened in your life – this is what prompted me to cross the border between the imaginary and the real world, my world and yours.

Thank goodness you didn't have the opportunity to kill your father or you would have regretted your action all your life. But that wasn't my main concern. What worried me the most was your inability to express yourself. You had shut yourself away from the world and I was afraid that you would jump or push the first nuisance from the heights of the mountains.

Thank goodness you had the courage to kiss Elodie or she would have had no reason to agree to leave everything behind for you and you probably would have continued to think you had to pay for wrongdoings you had not committed.

Victor, you have escaped death while it was after you.

Unfortunately, it took away your friend Jung. I've never been his brother. He would have liked to have one, he would have needed one, he imagined he had one. But he's never had a brother. I hoped that after you met at The Manor of Woe it would prevent two foretold tragedies. It's me who put that London address in his pocket, and when he gave it to you, it went the way I was hoping for, thinking that with the two of you in a foreign country, you would help each other. I tried to save him. He wasn't strong enough.

My mission, which is drawing to a close, was to make life worth living again for you, even if it meant temporarily sacrificing an entire village to achieve it.

Man is full of resources. Soon, the empty houses of Worsden Pane will be inhabited again, businesses will reopen and everyday life will resume. As for you, you will be responsible for the happiness of Elodie and for the future of your child.

Don't be afraid anymore. Elodie will soon be with you. I wish you all the happiness in the world.

Kimpôl.

As I finished reading, the file self-destructed. I stood for a moment, frozen in front of the computer. Then I turned it off. As Elodie had asked me, I packed the bags.

I heard a horn. The taxi was outside the door. Anxious to hold her in my arms, I went to meet Elodie…

Acknowledgements

Thanks to Jaid and Martina Mindang, Jean Pailler, Marianna Bettini Springfield, Marina Hardwick and Richard Sheehan.